THE BAY AT NICE
WRECKED EGGS

THE BAY AT NICE
WRECKED EGGS

DAVID HARE

faber and faber
LONDON · BOSTON

First published in 1986 by
Faber and Faber Limited
3 Queen Square London WC1N 3AU

Filmset by Wilmaset, Birkenhead, Wirral
Printed in Great Britain by
Cox & Wyman Ltd, Reading, Berkshire

British Library Cataloguing in Publication Data

Hare, David
Bay at Nice ; and, wrecked eggs.
I. Title II. Hare, David. Wrecked eggs
822'.914   PR6058.A678
ISBN 0–571–14694–5

for Blair

CONTENTS

THE BAY AT NICE

CHARACTERS

VALENTINA NROVKA
SOPHIA YEPILEVA
ASSISTANT CURATOR
PETER LINITSKY

The Bay at Nice and *Wrecked Eggs* were first performed at the Cottesloe Theatre, London, on 4 September 1986. The cast for *The Bay at Nice* was as follows:

VALENTINA NROVKA	Irene Worth
SOPHIA YEPILEVA	Zoë Wanamaker
ASSISTANT CURATOR	Colin Stinton
PETER LINITSKY	Philip Locke
Design	John Gunter
Lighting	Rory Dempster
Director	David Hare

The scene is set in Leningrad, 1956.

*A large room with a gilt ceiling and a beautiful parquet floor. At the
back hangs Guérin's huge oil painting of 'Iris and Morpheus', a
triumphant nude sitting on a cloud over the body of the King of
Sleep. The room is airy and decaying. It is almost empty but for
some tables pushed to the back and some gilt and red plush hard
chairs. Sitting on one of these is* VALENTINA NROVKA. *She is
a lively woman, probably in her sixties but it's hard to tell. She
is dressed in black. Her daughter* SOPHIA *is standing right at
the far end of the room looking out of the main door. She is in
her early thirties, much more plainly dressed in a coat and
pullover and plain skirt.*

VALENTINA: You don't want to leave an old woman.

SOPHIA: You're not old.

(VALENTINA *looks round disapprovingly.*)

VALENTINA: This graveyard! I'm not going to speak to all those
old idiots.

SOPHIA: They expect it.

VALENTINA: Nonsense! I'll sit by myself.

(SOPHIA *is still looking anxiously out of the door.*)

SOPHIA: I'm afraid we've offended the Curator.

VALENTINA: Don't say *we*. I offended him. He was shabbily
dressed.

SOPHIA: He wanted you to see the new extension.

VALENTINA: What for? He insults the walls by hanging them
with all that socialist realism. Whirlpools of mud. I'd rather
look at bare walls. At least they are cleanly painted. I'm
tired of looking anyway. 'Look, look . . .' (*She smiles,
anticipating her own story.*) Picasso lived in a house so ugly –
a great champagne millionaire's Gothic mansion with
turrets – that all his friends said 'My God, how can you
abide such a place?' He said, 'You are all prisoners of taste.
Great artists love everything. There is no such thing as
ugliness.' He would kick the walls with his little sandalled
foot and say, 'They're solid. What more do you want?'

5

SOPHIA: By that argument, if everything's beautiful, then that includes socialist realism.

VALENTINA: Please. You know nothing of such things. Don't speak of them. Especially in front of other people. It's embarrassing. (VALENTINA *has got up from her seat and is walking to the other side of the room.*) What rubbish do they want me to look at?

SOPHIA: They think they have a Matisse.

(*There is a silence.* VALENTINA *shows no apparent reaction.*)

VALENTINA: You haven't been to see me.

SOPHIA: No. I've been busy.

VALENTINA: Ah well.

SOPHIA: The work has been very hard. And the children. At the end of the day I'm too tired to do anything. I've said to my employers, as a woman I resent it.

VALENTINA: 'As a woman'?

SOPHIA: Yes.

VALENTINA: What does that mean?

SOPHIA: Well . . .

VALENTINA: This fashion for calling people women. Now always 'as a *woman*', they say. It was so much more fun when I was young and you could just be a person. Now everyone speaks 'on behalf'. 'On behalf of Soviet women . . .'

SOPHIA: I only meant that I have a family. I also have a job. That's all. And at the school I am taken advantage of.

VALENTINA: They take you for a fool. They know you can never say no.

(SOPHIA *is looking across at her back, trying to judge her mood.*)

SOPHIA: Who visits you?

VALENTINA: No one. The Troyanofskis of course. They are terrible people. Madam Troyanofski wants to start a salon. I've told her it's too late. All the artists are dead. The poets are moaners. And the playwrights are worse. Because they're exhausting. People run round the stage. It tires me. In their stories the minute hand is going round like crazy. But the hour hand never turns at all. (*She smiles.*) 'Ah well,'

6

she said, 'if there are no artists worth asking, we can always talk philosophy.' No thank you!

SOPHIA: She likes ideas.

VALENTINA: Yes, well, they're Jews. (*She shrugs.*) Tell me, who do you think I should be seeing? Name anyone in Leningrad who's worth an hour. A full hour.

SOPHIA: Well, of course I enjoy everybody's company. I find something good or interesting in everyone.

(VALENTINA *looks at her mistrustfully.*)

VALENTINA: Yes?

SOPHIA: Shall I get you something to drink?

VALENTINA: Where is this man?

SOPHIA: You frightened him.

VALENTINA: What? So much he's thinking of not showing me the painting?

SOPHIA: I'll go and see.

VALENTINA: No, stay. I want to talk to you.

(SOPHIA *stays, but* VALENTINA *makes no effort to talk.*)

SOPHIA: The twins both asked me to send you their love.

VALENTINA: How old are they?

SOPHIA: Eight.

VALENTINA: Then plainly you're lying. No eight-year-old asks after adults. Or if they do, they're faking. Why should your children fake?

SOPHIA: I said I would be seeing you and I suggested . . .

VALENTINA: Ah well, yes.

SOPHIA: . . . they send you their love.

VALENTINA: Now we get the truth of it. Their love was solicited. Like a confession.

SOPHIA: If you insist.

VALENTINA: And Grigor . . . what?

SOPHIA: Grigor is working. He would be here today.

VALENTINA: But?

SOPHIA: But he is working. And he's not interested in art.

VALENTINA: No.

(*There is a pause.* SOPHIA *looks away, as if anxious to say more, but not daring.*)

Where is the painting?

SOPHIA: They're getting it now. It's in a vault at the bottom of the building.

VALENTINA: Have you seen it?

SOPHIA: Not yet.

VALENTINA: What does it show?

SOPHIA: A window. The sea. A piece of wall.

VALENTINA: It sounds like a forgery.

SOPHIA: They think you will be able to tell.

VALENTINA: How can I tell? I don't know everything he painted. Nobody does. He got up every morning. He set up his easel and he started to paint. If at midday he was pleased, then he signed it. If not, then he threw it away and began fresh the next morning. It was said, like a dandy who throws white ties into the laundry basket until he ties one which pleases him. (*She smiles.*) Matisse was profligate.

SOPHIA: So there may be lost work?

VALENTINA: Well, of course. (*She turns away, contemptuously.*) And if there is, what will happen to it? They will put it on the walls of this hideous building. And the state will boast that they own it. And people will gawp at it and say 'What does it mean?' Or 'Well, I don't like it.' I am told that in the West now people only look at paintings when they are holding cubes of cheese on the end of toothpicks. To me, that says everything of what art has become. (*She smiles.*) Yes, indeed. I sympathize with Grigor. Why be interested in all this gossip and hoopla?

SOPHIA: No, you're wrong. It is painting itself which Grigor dislikes.

VALENTINA: Because you paint?

(SOPHIA *looks at her angrily.*)

SOPHIA: I shall look for the Curator.

VALENTINA: I have heard all these rumours. Even I. Who have no contact with life except through the Troyanofskis. They are my inadequate means of access to what is happening in the world. Through them everything is admittedly made mean. And yet. I have heard of your behaviour with Grigor.

SOPHIA: Mother, I don't want to speak about it now.

VALENTINA: Why?

SOPHIA: You will learn in a moment. Soon I shall talk to you.

VALENTINA: When?

SOPHIA: When I have your whole attention.

VALENTINA: Are you choosing your moment?

SOPHIA: No.

VALENTINA: It sums you up. You think everything is a matter of mood.

SOPHIA: I know you better than that.

VALENTINA: You think attitudes are all to do with whim. You understand nothing. Attitudes are all to do with character.

SOPHIA: Please don't lecture me. (*She is turning red with the effort of having to say this*.) If we are to speak we must speak as equals.

(VALENTINA *is looking across at her with sudden kindness and love*.)

VALENTINA: Little Sophia, you've used up all your courage already. Come here and tell me what's going on.

(SOPHIA, *trembling, doesn't move as* VALENTINA *opens her arms to her*.)

SOPHIA: No, I won't come. I mustn't. I'm determined to be strong with you.

VALENTINA: You've come to make a speech?

SOPHIA: Well, yes.

VALENTINA: Well, make it.

SOPHIA: What, now?

VALENTINA: Yes.

(*There is an agonizing pause*.)

SOPHIA: No, I can't.

VALENTINA: Why not?

SOPHIA: Because I have rehearsed but now I'm frightened. I've said these things to no one.

VALENTINA: And yet everyone knows.

(SOPHIA *does not move*.)

SOPHIA: I work. I am sober. I am honest. All day at that school. As you say, always extra duty. I stay long after class. Then

9

I go and stand in line in the shops. I look after the children. I offend no one. And yet if I even have a thought – a *thought* even – it's a crime. Everyone is waiting. Everyone stands ready to condemn me. (*She turns and suddenly rushes to the far side of the room.*) No, it's too cruel.

(*She is overwhelmed. She stands facing away from the room. Her mother does not turn. Then in the silence the* ASSISTANT CURATOR *comes in carrying a canvas which is facing towards him. He is in his mid-thirties. He wears a blue suit. He is nervous.*)

ASSISTANT: The painting is here.

VALENTINA: Where?

ASSISTANT: I have it. Madame Nrovka. (*He holds it out, a little puzzled, from the far side of the room.*)

VALENTINA: Put it down.

ASSISTANT: Where?

VALENTINA: Well, over there.

(*She gestures at a distant chair. He leans it on the chair, face turned away.*)

ASSISTANT: Will you view it?

VALENTINA: I will look at it later. I'm talking to my daughter.

SOPHIA: Forgive me. I'm appallingly rude. (*She wakes up to his embarrassment and walks over to shake his hand.*) I'm Sophia Yepileva.

ASSISTANT: I'm the Assistant Curator.

VALENTINA: No doubt your boss has sent you. He is too frightened himself.

ASSISTANT: I'm sorry?

VALENTINA: If he is frightened, why did he ask me? Why do you need me? Surely you have experts?

ASSISTANT: We do. Of all kinds.

VALENTINA: What do they say?

ASSISTANT: There is a slight problem. (*He looks nervously to* SOPHIA, *as if not liking them both to be there.*) How shall I put it? There are shades of a dispute. The scientific experts are used to handling *older* paintings.

VALENTINA: Yes, of course.

ASSISTANT: We know a great deal about pigment chronology. We have radio carbon. We have X-ray crystallography. We have wet chemistry. All these are invaluable if the painting is old enough. Because dating is what usually gives the forger away.

VALENTINA: But Matisse is too recent.

ASSISTANT: That's right. (*He smiles, nervous again.*) That is what we – who help run the museum – we are saying this to the scientists, you see. Who do not work for us. They work for the Ministry.

VALENTINA: Ah, well.

(*There is a pause as the* ASSISTANT *appreciates she has understood the problem, then he hurries on.*)

ASSISTANT: Their work is very useful. It is respected. Within certain limits. They have proved that if the canvas was forged, it was forged some time ago. Almost certainly in France. They can establish that. Where and when. That is useful work. But it does – in this case – we believe – stop short of *who*.

VALENTINA: Which you mean is much more a matter of taste.

ASSISTANT: Oh no . . . not entirely . . . (*He smiles reassuringly at her.*) There is circumstantial evidence. We can guess at motive. We are very suspicious. Obviously. Because Matisse is so recently dead. Only two years ago. If someone were trying – what? – to test the water, this would be an ideal moment. A forger usually offers a cycle of work.

VALENTINA: This would be the first.

ASSISTANT: Exactly. (*He looks to* SOPHIA.) Forgers usually can't resist. Once they have acquired a style, they're reluctant to let go of it.

VALENTINA: No different from painters. Except the very greatest.

ASSISTANT: Vrain Lucas forged manuscripts in the hands of Julius Caesar, the Apostle Paul and Joan of Arc. A bewildering diversity. But mercifully for us, exceptional.

VALENTINA: And what about the art critics?

ASSISTANT: Yes, a couple have also had a look.

VALENTINA: Well?

(*The* ASSISTANT *looks hopelessly.*)

ASSISTANT: Adjectives are so subjective, isn't that the problem? 'Over-decorative'. 'Too plastic', they say. 'Too cold'. 'Not fluid'. They mean one thing to one man, something quite different to another. (*He pauses a moment.*) So we thought to ask someone who knew the man himself.

(VALENTINA *shrugs this off.*)

VALENTINA: Surely many people knew him. He even visited this museum, I think.

ASSISTANT: I gather, yes. We were honoured. Some time before the war.

VALENTINA: So?

ASSISTANT: It was felt you understand his spirit.

VALENTINA: The experts concede that?

ASSISTANT: Well, no, actually . . .

(VALENTINA *smiles, her judgement confirmed.*)

Professor Satayev expressly forbade your being asked. He was against it. He has authenticated the painting, he insists. By scientific methods.

VALENTINA: (*Ironically*) Well then?

ASSISTANT: But if he were wrong it would be a major embarrassment.

VALENTINA: For whom?

(*There is a slight pause.*)

For whom?

(*The* ASSISTANT *looks nervously to* SOPHIA.)

You mean for the authorities?

ASSISTANT: Well, perhaps. Yes. For everyone.

VALENTINA: So the white witch is called in.

(*She smiles.* SOPHIA *looks uneasily at the* ASSISTANT.)

ASSISTANT: As you know, Matisse himself was fanatic. In his own lifetime. He would always go round to check the work being sold under his name. By an irony the letters of authentication he then wrote are in themselves incredibly valuable. They change hands at three thousand roubles.

One or two, we think, have already been forged. (*He
smiles*.) The whole business is way out of hand.

VALENTINA: He would be appalled.

SOPHIA: (*Frowns*) How do you decide? Finally?

ASSISTANT: There are tests. But these are all negative by
nature. They tell you if it cannot be Matisse. Dating,
pigment, brushwork, so on. If the negative tests are all
passed you are forced to conclude the work must be real.
The absence of disproof is finally proof. No one ever says
'Oh yes, this is his . . .' Except . . . (*He pauses*.)

SOPHIA: When?

ASSISTANT: Except when there's someone. I don't know . . .
when there's someone who knew him quite well.
(*There is a pause.* VALENTINA *seems uninterested, with
thoughts of her own*.)

SOPHIA: I see.

VALENTINA: My daughter is a painter.

ASSISTANT: Oh really? I'm afraid I don't know your work.

SOPHIA: My mother is exaggerating. I'm an amateur only.

VALENTINA: She tried to paint the sun.

SOPHIA: Yes, Mother.

VALENTINA: The sun can't be painted. Cézanne said, it can be
represented but it can't be reproduced. She tries to prove
Cézanne wrong.

SOPHIA: Yes, Mother, but I do it for pleasure.

VALENTINA: Pleasure!

SOPHIA: Yes. I sketch for myself. Not to be in competition with
great artists. You think we all want to be Cézanne. Why?

VALENTINA: You should want to be Cézanne. Or else why
paint?

SOPHIA: For enjoyment.

VALENTINA: That's nonsense. Painting must be learnt. Like
any other discipline. Why go in with no sense of what
others have achieved?

SOPHIA: I don't think like that. To me, that's not the point of
it.

VALENTINA: Then what is the point of it?

SOPHIA: I paint simply in order . . . (*She stops. Then rather feebly, as if knowing how lame it sounds:*) . . . to show what is there.

(VALENTINA *gestures, her case proved.*)

VALENTINA: That is why she can never be good. What you do is called photography. They said of Picasso that he couldn't paint a tree. They were wrong. He was painting trees when he was eight. It quickly came to bore him. He had no interest in trees after that. But he could paint the feeling you had when you looked at a tree. And that is more valuable. Painting is ultimately to do with the quality of feeling. That is why you will never be able to paint.

(*The* ASSISTANT *looks between the two women, embarrassed. But* SOPHIA *seems unfazed.*)

SOPHIA: (*Quietly*) I don't know.

ASSISTANT: I can't tell. I'm an Academician. My heart is in the catalogue.

SOPHIA: Ah, yes.

ASSISTANT: Matisse is a dauntingly complex subject. To be honest, I haven't lately looked at his paintings. I like them. I love them, in fact.

SOPHIA: Well then, marry them.

ASSISTANT: What?

SOPHIA: No, it's just . . .

(SOPHIA *is smiling. So is* VALENTINA. *A joke shared.*)

It's what my son says. I have twins. When my daughter's eating, say, chocolate cake, when she says 'I love this cake' . . . 'Well then, marry it.' That's what my son says.

(*There's a pause. The* ASSISTANT *seems bewildered, the women both amused.*)

ASSISTANT: If . . .

VALENTINA: What . . .

ASSISTANT: No . . .

SOPHIA: I'm sorry.

ASSISTANT: No, if . . .

SOPHIA: I'm just being silly.

VALENTINA: To get back to the subject.

ASSISTANT: Yes.

VALENTINA: Where was this found?

(*The* ASSISTANT *looks anxiously between them.*)

ASSISTANT: It belongs to a Count. A Tsarist.

VALENTINA: I see.

ASSISTANT: He left his home in 1919. He went to live in the South of France. He claims the canvas had been discarded in Matisse's hotel.

VALENTINA: In Nice?

ASSISTANT: Yes. In the Hotel de la Méditerranée. He was a friend of the manager's. The painting had been literally thrown out. I know it's hard to believe.

VALENTINA: I don't think so.

ASSISTANT: He never had it catalogued or valued because of the irregular way in which it was acquired. He was frightened his ownership would then be challenged.

VALENTINA: And how do you come to have it?

ASSISTANT: It's a bequest. The Count died earlier this year. In fact of a disease which has hitherto been diagnosed only in horses. A kind of horse flu, it turned out. The doctors thought he was medically unique.

VALENTINA: My goodness.

ASSISTANT: I mean, he raced a great deal. That's what he did in France all the time . . . all the time the rest of us were here. So to speak. The Count bred horses in the Midi.

(*There is a pause.*)

VALENTINA: I see.

ASSISTANT: The puzzling thing of course is, since he fled Russia, why he chose to leave us a painting of such value in his will.

VALENTINA: That puzzles you?

ASSISTANT: Yes. Not you?

VALENTINA: No. (*She is suddenly very quiet.*) You've not lived abroad.

ASSISTANT: Well, no . . .

VALENTINA: I was some time in Paris. Oh, many years ago. Before the revolution.

ASSISTANT: Yes, I know.

VALENTINA: It can pall. Being away. Believe me.

ASSISTANT: Yes, I'm sure.

VALENTINA: We must all make our peace.

ASSISTANT: You mean the Count has made his? By an act of generosity?

SOPHIA: Yes. Or else he's sold you a pup.

(*The women smile. The* ASSISTANT *looks discomfited.*)

VALENTINA: Well, that's right.

SOPHIA: I don't understand the legal position. If the Count stole it.

ASSISTANT: 'Stole'? I wouldn't say 'stole'.

SOPHIA: Picked it up.

ASSISTANT: He acquired it.

SOPHIA: Legitimately?

ASSISTANT: Oh, well, really . . . (*He suddenly becomes expansive.*) Apart from anything, so much time has gone by. All art is loot. Who should own it? I shouldn't say this, but there isn't much justice in these things. If we examined the process whereby everything on these walls was acquired . . . we should have bare walls.

SOPHIA: My mother was just saying how much she would prefer that.

VALENTINA: Come, what does it show?

(*The* ASSISTANT *makes as if to go and pick it up.*)

No, tell me.

ASSISTANT: Well, it's like a sketch – I'm not speaking technically . . .

VALENTINA: No, I understand.

ASSISTANT: I mean a kind of dry-run. For everything that follows. Except the foreground is bare. There is no woman. There is no violin. There is no chair. (*He shrugs.*) There is just a wall. A pair of curtains. Wallpaper. Open windows. The sea. (*There is a sudden silence. Then he shrugs again.*) It is either a copy. Or a beginning.

VALENTINA: Yes. (*She pauses a moment, then she speaks with great finality, as if finishing a poem.*) He did them. Then he

threw them away. (*She gets up from her chair and walks to the far side of the room, where she addresses the* ASSISTANT.)
You may bring me some tea.

ASSISTANT: Well, I will. I shall leave you some time with the painting. Alone.

(*He looks a moment to* SOPHIA *who does not move*.)

I am very grateful. And the Curator, I think, would be grateful too for your subsequent discretion. Our scientists must not be upset.

(*The* ASSISTANT *smiles and goes out. The women do not move*.)

VALENTINA: He's a weak man.

SOPHIA: Yes.

VALENTINA: He doesn't give a fig about painting.

SOPHIA: Do you need time?

(VALENTINA *turns and looks her straight in the eye, level. Then she turns away*.)

VALENTINA: No. I already know.

(*There is a pause*. VALENTINA *deep in thought*, SOPHIA *watching her*.)

Make your speech.

SOPHIA: What?

VALENTINA: I am ready.

SOPHIA: Now?

VALENTINA: Yes. Isn't that why you're here?

SOPHIA: No. I wanted to come with you. I was interested.

VALENTINA: You want to leave Grigor.

(SOPHIA *hesitates a moment*.)

SOPHIA: How do you know?

VALENTINA: You've wanted to leave since the moment you were married.

SOPHIA: That's not true.

VALENTINA: What else could it be? But now I can see you are hardening. You have the will. It's there. I sense it in you. You have become determined.

SOPHIA: First I want to talk to you.

VALENTINA: Don't lie. Please don't lie. I can tell you've made up your mind. Haven't you?

(SOPHIA *does not answer.*)

Sophia, please. Talk to me properly.

SOPHIA: Yes.

(*There's a pause.* VALENTINA *is very quiet.*)

VALENTINA: Then I am sure you've met another man.

(SOPHIA *looks down.*)

SOPHIA: Yes.

VALENTINA: You're in love.

SOPHIA: I think less and less of love. What does love have to do with it? What matters is not love, but what the other person makes you. (SOPHIA *turns and walks away to the far side of the room.*) When I stand next to Grigor, it's clear, he is a dutiful man. He's a model servant of the State. Next to him, I look only like a fortunate woman who must struggle every day to deserve the luck she's had in marrying someone so worthwhile. That is my role. In marriages everyone gets cast. The strong one, the weak. The quick one, the slow. The steady, the giddy. It's set. Almost from the moment you meet. You don't notice it, you take it for granted, you think you're just *you*. Fixed, unchangeable. But you're not. You're what you've been cast as with the other person. And it's all got nothing to do with who you really are.

VALENTINA: Nothing?

SOPHIA: With Grigor, I'm dowdy, I'm scatterbrained, I'm trying to prove myself. All the standards are his. Grigor, of course, has nothing to prove. He's a headmaster at thirty-seven, the Party approves of him. He can always find his shirts in the drawer. I usually can. But Usually is no good next to Always. 'Usually' becomes a great effort of will. All I can do . . . no, all I can *be* is an inadequate, minor commentary on Grigor's far more finished character. Grigor and Sophia. After ten years we each have our part. Whereas when I'm with . . . this other man . . . then suddenly I'm quite someone else.

(*There is a pause.*)

VALENTINA: He is a less good man, I assume from what you're saying . . .

SOPHIA: Oh no, it's not as easy as that.

VALENTINA: He is less of a challenge, is that right?

SOPHIA: No!

VALENTINA: You've found yourself a mediocrity, so you suffer less by comparison. Is that what you mean?

SOPHIA: Not at all.

VALENTINA: Well, is it? (*She asks this with sudden emphasis. She waits, then getting no reply, laughs.*) What does he do, this other person with no name?

SOPHIA: He works for the Sanitation Board.

VALENTINA: Well, exactly!

(SOPHIA *is pointing at her, bright red with anger.*)

SOPHIA: Mother, if you prevent me, I will never forgive you.

VALENTINA: Me? What can I do?

SOPHIA: Withhold your approval.

VALENTINA: My approval?

SOPHIA: Yes.

VALENTINA: From an empty room you never visit?

SOPHIA: I visit you.

VALENTINA: You visit occasionally. Would you really miss that?

(SOPHIA *is exasperated.*)

SOPHIA: You don't even like Grigor.

VALENTINA: Well . . .

SOPHIA: It's true. You never did. From the start. You said he was a prig.

VALENTINA: What do I matter? It's not me you have to fear. If you don't know by now, you must face your own conscience. Your children.

SOPHIA: Do you think I've not thought of them? Mother, it's hard. But I have the right to live my own life.

(VALENTINA *turns away, smiling.*)

VALENTINA: Oh, rights.

SOPHIA: No doubt by will . . . by some great effort of will our marriage may be saved. By will, we may grow old together. But I remember once you said to me: nothing's worth having by will.

VALENTINA: Did I say that?

(SOPHIA *looks at her, then moves away, shaking her head.*)

SOPHIA: And anyway, it's wrong. There's a principle.

VALENTINA: Oh, really?

SOPHIA: Yes.

VALENTINA: You still believe in that?

SOPHIA: Of course. What do you mean? In their private life, a person must be free to live as they choose.

(VALENTINA *raises her eyebrows.*)

VALENTINA: My goodness me, your principles are convenient. You call that an ideal?

SOPHIA: Forgive me but I'm afraid . . . yes, well I do.

VALENTINA: How convenient. Goodness. An ideal. Which also coincides with what you want. How perfect. What perfect luck. Run off with this man. Call it 'living my own life'. 'I must be myself, I must do what I want . . .' (*She smiles.*) I have heard these words before. On boulevards. In cafés. I used to hear them in Paris. I associate them with zinc tables and the gushing of beer. Everyone talking about their entitlements. 'I must be allowed to realize myself.' For me, it had a different name. I never called it principle. I called it selfishness.

SOPHIA: How can you say that to me?

VALENTINA: Oh yes. Men – your father's friends – used these very same words. Many times. When I was pregnant they said 'Get rid of it. You must live your own life. A child will burden you. You have a right to be happy. Get on with your painting, and realize yourself.' You owe your very existence to the fact I did not choose to live my own life.

SOPHIA: Yes, but that's different . . .

VALENTINA: No, not at all. It's what's involved in facing up to being an adult. Sacrifice and discipline and giving yourself to others, not always thinking of yourself, and sometimes . . . yes . . . being harsh. As I am being harsh . . .

SOPHIA: Oh, how you love that harshness. Nothing can ever be harsh enough for you.

(VALENTINA *turns away, but* SOPHIA *does not relent.*)
Well, that's not my fault. It's your fault. You like

responsibility? I give it you. It was your fault. It was your life you ruined. You did it. All by yourself. Without consultation. (*She turns away.*) Well, I'm not going to let you now ruin mine.

(*Standing at the open door of the room now is* PETER LINITSKY. *He is in his mid-sixties, he is bald, he has an unremarkable blue overcoat and carries his hat in his hand. His manner is apologetic.*)

PETER: Excuse me.

SOPHIA: Oh God.

PETER: Am I interrupting?

SOPHIA: No, no, come in.

VALENTINA: Please go away. Who is this?

SOPHIA: It's him.

VALENTINA: What do you mean?

(VALENTINA *is genuinely taken aback by* PETER's *age and his appearance.*)

SOPHIA: It's Peter.

VALENTINA: Peter?

SOPHIA: Yes, Peter, for God's sake. Wake up, Mother. The man with no name.

VALENTINA: It's him?

SOPHIA: Yes.

PETER: What?

SOPHIA: Yes. Goodness. How many times?

PETER: What do you mean, no name?

SOPHIA: Forget it.

VALENTINA: Are you with the Sanitation Board?

PETER: Well, I . . .

SOPHIA: Leave it. You know he is. Don't answer, Peter.

PETER: I didn't get the chance.

SOPHIA: Don't play her game. She contrives to make the words sound like an insult.

PETER: If you . . .

VALENTINA: What words?

SOPHIA: Sanitation Board.

VALENTINA: Did I?

(SOPHIA *suddenly turns to her mother with surprising force*.)

SOPHIA: Down here below you, people are forced to be
ridiculous. Yes. We lead ridiculous lives. Doing ridiculous
things, which lack taste. Like working for a living. For
organizations which have ridiculous names. 'Oh, I'm from
the Department of Highway Cleansing.' 'Oh, I'm
Vegetation Officer in Minsk.' That's work. It's called
making a living, Mother, it involves silly names and
unspeakable people – the mathematics teacher, for me to
work beside her, to have lunch, to watch her pick her dirty
grey hair from the soup, it's torture, I'd rather lodge beside
an open drain. But that's how people live. We have to. We
scrabble about in the real world. Because we don't sit
thinking all day about art.

(VALENTINA *turns bitterly to* PETER.)

VALENTINA: Is she like this with you?

SOPHIA: Don't answer.

VALENTINA: Peter?

PETER: Like what?

VALENTINA: Self-righteous.

PETER: Er, no.

SOPHIA: Would you two like to be introduced?

VALENTINA: Not specially.

PETER: Good afternoon.

SOPHIA: His name is Peter Linitsky. My mother.

PETER: At last.

VALENTINA: I feel I already know you. Do you have a wife?

SOPHIA: Say nothing.

PETER: I did.

(*There is a pause. Finally* PETER *feels compelled to fill it in*.)
She is an extraordinary woman.

VALENTINA: I'm sure. Now you're rid of her. Leningrad is full
of ageing men praising their wives. Whom they have
invariably left. If you hear a man praise his wife in Russia,
it means they are no longer together.

SOPHIA: Peter left six years ago.

VALENTINA: Peter left?

22

PETER: No, seven.

VALENTINA: Oh, seven is one better, of course. Don't miss one. Each one counts. Doesn't each one make it more respectable?

PETER: I have a divorce.

VALENTINA: Well done. It's hard.

SOPHIA: Divorce is possible.

VALENTINA: Yes.

(*There is a pause. Nobody moves.*)

SOPHIA: Mother, it's possible.

VALENTINA: Yes.

(VALENTINA *looks at her a moment, with the calm of someone who suddenly knows they have an unanswerable argument.*)

Peter, I know nothing about you. For all I know, you're a kind and decent man. I'm sure you managed a divorce. But I am sure . . . I would stake my life . . . you are not in the Party.

(*There is a silence.*)

PETER: No.

(VALENTINA *nods very slightly, acknowledging the admission.* SOPHIA *looks between them. Quietly:*)

SOPHIA: Mother, neither am I.

(VALENTINA *looks at her steadily.*)

I have already written to the paper. To place an advertisement.

VALENTINA: Does Grigor know?

SOPHIA: No.

VALENTINA: It means nothing. When did you write?

(*She doesn't answer.*)

PETER: She wrote a week ago.

VALENTINA: How long will it take?

PETER: The waiting-list is nine months, to get your item in. At the moment. Some people have waited a year.

VALENTINA: Nine months for the advertisement?

PETER: That's right. Unless . . .

VALENTINA: What?

SOPHIA: (*Finishing for him*) . . . it can be brought forward.

VALENTINA: What? Are you thinking of moving out of
Leningrad?

(PETER *and* SOPHIA *look at one another.*)

SOPHIA: No . . .

PETER: We . . .

SOPHIA: No, there are towns, we know of towns . . . not far
away . . . where the queue is not so long for the local paper.
And the papers there give more space. A month. Two
months. But you must prove residency. You must room
there. And . . . there's no question . . . Peter can't leave his
job.

PETER: (*Smiles*) No money.

SOPHIA: And I can't leave mine. I can't take the children.

VALENTINA: Well, here they won't print it. They will ask
Grigor first.

SOPHIA: That's not the law.

VALENTINA: They will ask him. He won't agree to publication.
Let alone to all the Court procedures which follow.

SOPHIA: It doesn't matter. I still have the right.

(VALENTINA *suddenly gets angry.*)

VALENTINA: Don't use that word. You have the *right*? What
does it mean? It doesn't mean anything. Be a person. Do
what you have to. Don't prattle about rights.

(SOPHIA *looks to* PETER *for support.*)

SOPHIA: Mother, there are ways. It can be speeded.

VALENTINA: I've never heard of it.

SOPHIA: If you spoke to Grigor.

VALENTINA: If *I* spoke?

SOPHIA: Yes.

VALENTINA: Is this what you came here to ask me?

SOPHIA: If you said you'd seen me . . . and you knew how
deeply I felt. You know what the legal criterion is for
divorce? It's quite simple. The criterion for divorce is
necessity.

(*There is a pause.*)

Mother, I need to be free.

(VALENTINA *smiles. Lightly:*)

24

VALENTINA: Grigor's not free. You're not free. Child, you've lived thirty-six years. How can you be so naïve?

SOPHIA: Is it naïve?

VALENTINA: Of course. There's no freedom.

SOPHIA: Oh, really? That's not what I've heard.

VALENTINA: Where? Where do you think there is freedom?

SOPHIA: Well, I've always heard . . . from what you say of Paris . . .

VALENTINA: Don't be ridiculous.

SOPHIA: Your life there.

VALENTINA: I was seventeen!

SOPHIA: With . . . how many lovers? My mother always told me . . .

(*She turns to* PETER.)

PETER: Goodness.

SOPHIA: While she was meant to be learning to draw.

VALENTINA: That was Paris. (*She pauses, as if protecting a memory.*) Paris was different.

SOPHIA: Oh, I see. And is Paris the only place where people may be happy? (*She waits a moment. Then quietly:*) Or is it just you who wants it that way?

(*There is a silence.* SOPHIA *waits. But* VALENTINA *just seems amused.*)

VALENTINA: I see. And you think freedom is happiness, do you?

(SOPHIA *doesn't answer.*)

You think it's the same thing? Do you, Peter?

PETER: Well I . . . I don't know. I'm pressed to make a living. Half goes to my ex-wife. My children are grown-up. They work in a factory making bottles. One's doing quite well. The other was born a bit slow. So I am always thinking of him. Most days. Most hours. (*He smiles thinly.*) I'm not an expert on freedom.

VALENTINA: Yes, well, you're wiser than her.

(PETER *looks a little nervously to* SOPHIA.)

PETER: I only know I've not had much luck in things. I find myself nearly sixty-three. And . . . never really had the chance to take a risk in my life. What else is there now for me but Sophia? I don't mean it unkindly but . . . well, I live alone, I have a room, I'm a great lover of walking, I meet in the park with other model aircraft collectors . . .

SOPHIA: His aircraft are beautiful.

PETER: No, they're . . . quite average. But without Sophia I might as well die. (*He takes another look at her.*)

VALENTINA: You didn't think that before?

PETER: What do you mean?

VALENTINA: Before you met her?

PETER: No. I mean, no. Hardly. How could I? But I think it now.

VALENTINA: Well, that's love for you, isn't it? Before you met her you were happy.

PETER: Not happy, no.

VALENTINA: But not 'Oh, I'll die'. (*She suddenly raises her voice.*) You're Stravinsky's grandfather.

PETER: I don't understand.

VALENTINA: Stravinsky's grandfather died trying to scale the garden fence on his way to an assignation with his mistress. He was a hundred and eleven years old at the time.
(PETER *smiles.* VALENTINA *laughs. Only* SOPHIA *is not amused.*)

SOPHIA: Don't say that of Peter.

VALENTINA: And what . . . what anyway . . . (*She moves suddenly and decisively on to the attack.*) What if you succeeded? What if she uses you to get her a divorce?

SOPHIA: I'm not doing that.

VALENTINA: What then?

PETER: What do you mean?

VALENTINA: Love is pain. Am I right?
(*He looks mistrustfully, fearing a trap.*)

PETER: Not entirely.

VALENTINA: Look at you now. You're in torture. You shift from one foot to another . . .

PETER: Well, I . . .

VALENTINA: You're forever taking sidelong glances at her,

checking up on her, seeing she approves of everything you say. Thinking all the time, how does this go down with Sophia? In fiction it makes me laugh when books end with two people coming together. Curtain! At last they fall into one another's arms! The reader applauds. But that's where books should really begin. (*She smiles.*) This fantasy that love solves problems! Love makes you raw. It strips the skin from you. Am I right?

PETER: In part.

VALENTINA: Suddenly everything has to matter so much. Really, who cares? Suddenly to be aware, to be prey to every exaggerated detail, every nuance of someone else's feelings. How demeaning! What possible point? And then what? What in the future? What will you do? Spend two years in the courts? Two years of little sidelong glances, and oh, is it all right? Is she weakening? Do I love her? Does she love me? And at the end, what? You'll suddenly realize – not a plateau. Oh no. Not safety. Not if it's love. Really love. Just as likely agony. Oh yes. A pure gambler's throw. And for this? For *this*? Chuck out everything. Husband. Jobs. Children. Grigor. Yes. Destroy Grigor's life. For a bet placed by two shivering tramps at the racetrack. (*She leans forward.*) And there's nothing guaranteed at the end. (*She gets up, her case proved.*) People should stick. They should stick with what they have. With what they know. That's character.

SOPHIA: You think so?

VALENTINA: Certainly. But these days people just can't wait to give up.

(SOPHIA *smiles, as if not threatened by any of this.*)

You make such a fuss about everything. I just get on with it. I know what life is. And what it cannot be.

(PETER *is puzzled by* SOPHIA's *calm. Now* VALENTINA *insults him aimlessly, with no real feeling.*)

You're a silly bald man. You're old and you're bald. Your shirt is too young for you. Your trousers are absurd. Is there anything worse than men who can't grow old with dignity? (*She sits at the side of the room, the storm blown out.*) I was promised tea. (*She suddenly shouts, as if she can't think of anything else to say.*) They promised me tea.

PETER: I will get it for you.

SOPHIA: No. Let me go.

(*She smiles and goes out.* PETER *is left standing near the canvas,* VALENTINA *sitting.*)

VALENTINA: She's a good girl. There's no harm in her. She's just weak. And talentless. Her father was a soldier. I knew him three weeks. He claimed there was a war. What did I know? He said his battalion had to move. Perhaps it was true. I never saw his battalion. He said the French had a war to go to in Abyssinia. I've never checked. Was there such a thing?

PETER: I've never heard of it.

VALENTINA: There's no way to tell.

PETER: This was in Paris?

VALENTINA: Yes. Paris and Leningrad. It's all I've known.

(PETER *waits a moment.*)

PETER: You must have met everyone. I mean, the famous.

VALENTINA: Certainly not. It wasn't like that. I had no interest. I once was asked to a party to meet Ford Madox Ford.

PETER: There you are.

VALENTINA: Him I had heard of. Because they said he was the least frequently washed of all modern novelists. So I didn't go. (*She shakes her head.*)

People get it wrong. They have no idea of it. Remember, we were poor. We had no ambitions for ourselves. At school we were a strange group. All penniless. Hungarians, a Chinese, some Americans. Well, Americans have money, but no one else. One boy wanted to pose in the life class. He was one of us. He needed to make money. He said 'Well, why not?' All day we looked at naked people. Men, women. 'You're not embarrassed,' he said, 'people come in, take their clothes off. It's fine. Why not me? Why not give me the money?' But we all had a meeting. We said no. A line would be crossed. (*She pauses, deep in thought.*) A naked stranger is one thing. But one of us naked – no. It's all wrong.

(PETER *waits respectfully*.)

PETER: This was an art school?

VALENTINA: School of painting. At the Sacred Heart Convent. In the Boulevard des Invalides.

PETER: Who taught you?

VALENTINA: A man who said he wanted to turn his lambs into lions.

PETER: Who was that?

VALENTINA: Henri Matisse.

(*There is a pause*.)

PETER: Matisse?

VALENTINA: Yes.

PETER: You mean Matisse?

VALENTINA: I said Matisse.

PETER: Yes, I know.

VALENTINA: Why, you admire him?

PETER: Just the idea that he was alive. And he taught you. It seems unbelievable.

VALENTINA: Well, it's a fact.

PETER: I didn't know he taught.

VALENTINA: He taught for three years.

PETER: Then?

(*She turns and looks at him*.)

VALENTINA: Then he didn't teach any more.

(PETER *looks down a moment*.)

PETER: You mean . . . look, I know nothing – art! – but I've seen some things he's done . . . but what I mean, did he feel there was no point to teaching?

VALENTINA: How would I know? He taught us rules. He believed in them. Not Renaissance rules. Those he was very against. He disliked Leonardo. Because of all that measuring. He said that was when art began to go wrong. When it became obsessed with measuring. Trying to establish how things work. It doesn't matter how they work. You can't *see* with a caliper. (*She smiles*.) Of course there were rules. He was a classicist. This is what no one understood. He disliked in modern painting the way one part is emphasized – the nose, or the foot, or the breast. He hated this distortion. He said you should always aim for the whole. Remember your first impression and stick to it. Balance nature and your view. Don't let your view run away of its own accord. For everything he did there was always a reason. No one saw this to begin with. On the walls of Paris, people painted slogans: Matisse is absinthe, Matisse drives you mad. But to meet, he was a German schoolmaster with little gold-rimmed glasses.

PETER: I've seen those drawings he did of himself. I like him in the mirror when he's drawing a nude.

VALENTINA: Yes, it's witty.

(*There is a pause.*)

Even with colour . . . the colours were so striking, people thought, why is this face blue? This is modern. But it wasn't. Each colour depends on what is placed next to it. One tone is just a colour. Two tones are a chord, which is life. (*She turns a moment, thoughtfully.*) It was the same with the body. No line exists on its own. Only with its relation to another do you create volume. He said you should think of the body as an architect does. The foot is a bridge. Arms are like rolls of clay. Forearms are like ropes, since they can be knotted and twisted. In drawing a head never leave out the ear. Adjust the different parts to each other. Each is dissimilar and yet must add to the whole. A tree is like a human body. A body is like a cathedral. (*She smiles.*) His models were always very beautiful. Sometimes he worked with the same model for years. No one drew the body better than him. The lines of a woman's stomach. The pudenda. A few curls. He could make you think of bed. And yet when he was working he said, he took a woman's clothes off and put them back on as if he were arranging a vase of flowers.

(*There is a pause.*)

He loved going to the mountains. When he was tired, he

said it was a relief. Because it's impossible to paint them. You can't paint a mountain. The scale is all wrong.

PETER: That's funny.

(*She looks at him, suddenly resuming her original answers.*)

VALENTINA: As to teaching, yes, of course, his teaching was inspiring. But it was as if Shakespeare had taught. It gave you an idea. But then when you pick up your own brush, you're faced with the reality of your own talent.

PETER: Frustrating?

VALENTINA: Not always. But how do I say? It's a very different thing. Talking is easy. Oh yes, and Matisse could talk. But genius is different.

(PETER *frowns a moment.*)

PETER: Did it depress you?

VALENTINA: No. I went on painting. Although I knew my limitations. I painted by will.

PETER: By will?

VALENTINA: Yes.

PETER: It's odd.

VALENTINA: What?

PETER: Last night, now, Sophia used that same phrase. 'By will.'

VALENTINA: Yes. She used it to me. (*She looks at him a moment.*) He taught a few years, then he went travelling. He went to Italy, Algeria, Tangiers. By then he was yet more famous. He'd given Picasso one of his paintings. Picasso's friends, who were all very stupid and malicious, used it as a dartboard. But it didn't matter. Matisse's reputation was made. He bought a house in Clamart. People mocked him because it had such a big bathroom. On the ground floor. Too much contact with Americans, that's what people said. He'd developed an interest in personal hygiene. But it wasn't true. Matisse was always clean. (*She smiles.*) I went there a couple of times. Madame Matisse used to cook. She served a jugged hare which was better than anything in Europe. And with it, a wine called Rančio. It's a sort of Madeira. Heavy but excellent. I've never had it since.

PETER: I don't know it.

VALENTINA: Years later in Berlin, he went for a great exhibition of his work. And waiting for him was the most enormous laurel wreath. 'To Henri Matisse, *cher maître* . . .' or whatever. He said, 'Why do you give me a wreath? I'm not dead.' But Madame Matisse plucked a leaf and tasted it. She said, 'This will make the most wonderful soup.'
(*There is a pause.*)

PETER: Yes.

VALENTINA: It was all one progress. I can't explain. I lost touch with him. I think everyone did. He simply moved out of all our lives. Yet whenever I heard later stories, they fitted. With him, everything belonged.

PETER: I can see that.

VALENTINA: I've seen photographs of him when he was dying. He's painting on his walls with a brush tied to the end of a long stick. He's too frail to move from his pillows. It's the same man I knew almost fifty years ago. (*She smiles.*) There was only one little – oh – what? – one tiny denial. Which was love. He told me he was too busy. To think of love properly. I mean, to explore it. No, he said. I have no time for that.

PETER: I find that strange.

VALENTINA: He was asked by an American journalist how many children he had. Four, he said. What are their names? Let me see. There's Marguerite. And Jean. And Pierre. He said suddenly, 'No, I have three.'

PETER: But isn't that . . .

VALENTINA: What?

PETER: A bit callous?

VALENTINA: I think it's admirable.

PETER: Why?

VALENTINA: Priorities!
(PETER *smiles.*)

PETER: It seems a bit chilly to me.

VALENTINA: He loved his family. He painted faces above his bed. He said he slept badly, but he always felt better if he could imagine his grandchildren. So he put them on the ceiling above him. That way he said, 'I feel less alone.'

PETER: But what did they feel?

VALENTINA: Does it matter? Marguerite was tortured by the Gestapo. She was in the Resistance. When she came home and told him, he couldn't paint for two weeks. Then he abandoned the work he'd been doing when he heard. Her pain was real to him. He was in anguish. But he could not incorporate her suffering. He didn't want to. He went on painting in just the same way.

(*There is a pause.*)

PETER: What about you?

VALENTINA: Me?

PETER: Were you like that? Disciplined?

VALENTINA: Good Lord, no. No. I wasted my time. Love was *all* I had time for. At least until the twenties.

PETER: Sophia said . . . (*He pauses.*)

VALENTINA: Yes?

PETER: She suggested . . . that for some reason you decided to come home.

VALENTINA: That's right. (*She waits.*) What else did she say?

PETER: No, nothing, just . . . she said, you didn't have to.

VALENTINA: I didn't have to. It was a choice of my own.

(*There is a pause.* PETER *waits.*)

I didn't know Matisse well. But I understood him. I understood what's called his handwriting. I love this phrase. Do you know what it is?

PETER: No.

VALENTINA: It's a painting term. Which is indefinable. It's not quite even signature. It's more than that. It's spirit.

(*She looks at him a moment, then* SOPHIA *returns, silently, with tea in a pot and cups on a tray. She moves round.*)

SOPHIA: Here's tea.

VALENTINA: Well, thank you.

SOPHIA: Everyone's vanished. The museum's closed.

VALENTINA: Already?

SOPHIA: It's dark now.

VALENTINA: I didn't notice. What have you done with the
    Assistant Curator?

SOPHIA: I told him to wait. (SOPHIA *gives her tea*.)

VALENTINA: Thank you. You've been talking of me, I gather,
    to Peter here.

SOPHIA: Not in particular. Do you want tea?

PETER: No, thank you.

SOPHIA: We're always short of time. Me and Linitsky.
    (*She smiles affectionately at him*.)
    We meet in a café far from our homes. Most of the time we
    talk about how to meet next. Then when we meet next,
    how to meet next. And so on.

VALENTINA: It sounds most exhausting.

SOPHIA: In China they say if you want to be taught by a
    particular professor, you must go to his door every day and
    ask to be a pupil. And every day for a year, two years, three
    years, he will close the door in your face. Then one day he
    will suddenly accept you. He's been testing your
    endurance. To see if you want the thing badly enough.

VALENTINA: What a sentimental notion.

SOPHIA: It's true.

VALENTINA: I'm sure it's true. (*The hardness of her tone suddenly
    returns*.) And meanwhile your life has gone by.
    (SOPHIA *looks a moment to* PETER.)

SOPHIA: So what did you decide?

PETER: Sorry?

SOPHIA: The two of you.

PETER: Oh. (*He pauses*.) About what?

SOPHIA: Peter . . .

PETER: Oh, I see.

SOPHIA: I'm asking, will my mother help us?

PETER: I don't know. She didn't say.
    (VALENTINA *smiles to herself*.)
    We didn't get on to the subject. To be honest, we were
    talking about art.

SOPHIA: Oh God.

PETER: I know.

SOPHIA: Really, Peter. I asked you . . .

PETER: I know. I'm ashamed.

VALENTINA: Did you give him a mission?

PETER: I got distracted, that's all.

VALENTINA: What was he meant to be asking me?

SOPHIA: (*To* VALENTINA) Nothing. Mind your own business.
(*To* PETER) Really! Do I have to do everything myself? (*She
is at once contrite.*) Oh God, I'm sorry.

PETER: No, no . . .

SOPHIA: Forgive me, I didn't mean to be unpleasant.

PETER: You're not being unpleasant. Really.

SOPHIA: I'm sorry, Peter.

PETER: No, it's my fault.

VALENTINA: Is this how your home life will be? God help us. I
think you'd both be better off on your own.

SOPHIA: Well, perhaps. (*She turns to* PETER.) What do you say?

PETER: No, I don't think so. For me it's an adventure, you see.
At last something's happening. Even if, as you say, it's
unbelievably uncomfortable. It uncovers feelings I didn't
know I had. (*He smiles, nervously.*) For a start, I'm jealous.
It's illogical. Jealous of the past. Of the life Sophia had
before I even knew her. The further back, the worse. Even
the idea . . . when I think of her as young . . . just young
. . . in a short gingham dress, on a pavement, with a
satchel, going to school, the idea of her life as an
eight-year-old fills my heart with such terrible longing.
Such a sense of loss. It makes no sense, it's ridiculous. My
brain reels, I can hardly think. Images of someone I never
even knew have a power to disturb me, to hurt me in a way
which is more profound than anything I've known. (*He
looks hopelessly to* VALENTINA.) What can I do? Just
abandon her?

SOPHIA: No.

PETER: Just say, 'Well, that's it. You've had your glimpse. Now
go home and do nothing but glue balsa wood on your own'?
(*He shrugs.*) Plainly it's true, I'm not happy. I'm what the
textbooks call 'seriously disturbed'. I wish I were stronger.

I wish she didn't so upset me. (*A pause.*) But I think I have to go on.

(*There is silence.* SOPHIA *looks at him a moment.*)

VALENTINA: I don't know. Why is that?

PETER: Why?

VALENTINA: Yes, why?

SOPHIA: He just told you.

VALENTINA: Yes. But what he feels will have an effect. On Grigor. On the children.

PETER: I love the children.

SOPHIA: They will live with us.

VALENTINA: Will they? And when will you tell them about the separation?

(SOPHIA *does not answer.*)

Sophia?

SOPHIA: I already have.

VALENTINA: What?

SOPHIA: Yes. I told them.

VALENTINA: Why did you do that?

SOPHIA: I felt it would be honest.

VALENTINA: Please don't lie to me.

PETER: Sophia . . .

SOPHIA: Also . . .

PETER: (*To* VALENTINA) I didn't know.

VALENTINA: Tell me your true reason.

SOPHIA: Many things.

VALENTINA: Such as?

(*There is a pause.*)

SOPHIA: There would be no going back.

(PETER *is looking across at her, alarmed.* VALENTINA *nods slightly.*)

VALENTINA: Yes. And Grigor? Was Grigor there?

SOPHIA: No. He wasn't with me. I did it this morning. He'll be home about now.

VALENTINA: You told them without asking him.

SOPHIA: Look, Mother, I've asked him often. He always says no. But they must know eventually.

VALENTINA: You told them without his permission?

SOPHIA: He will never give his permission. He claims I'm in the grip of a decadent fantasy. He says I am inflamed by the morals of the West. Mother, he's mad.

VALENTINA: The children won't love you. They will never forgive you.

(SOPHIA *is shaking her head, now very agitated.*)

SOPHIA: All right, I'll be there. I'll go home now. I'll tell him. I'll say 'Grigor, the children now know what you and I know.' I broke the news because if I didn't, nothing would have happened. Was that wrong? (*She suddenly cries out.*) Mother, don't look at me like that.

VALENTINA: What did the twins say?

SOPHIA: Well . . .

VALENTINA: Tell me.

SOPHIA: Look, what d'you think? Of course it isn't easy.

VALENTINA: Well?

SOPHIA: It's a long process. It's years.

VALENTINA: Just today?

(SOPHIA *pauses a moment.*)

SOPHIA: Nikolai was fine. At once he went back to playing. Alexandra said, would I please go away?

VALENTINA: She's *eight*.

SOPHIA: Mother, don't torture me.

(VALENTINA *turns to* PETER.)

VALENTINA: Peter, are you shocked?

PETER: No. (*He pauses, uncertain.*) Of course not. It had to be done. Eventually.

VALENTINA: Is there anything worse? Is there anything worse than the weak when they try to be strong? They make such a job of it!

PETER: That isn't fair.

VALENTINA: Oh, I see. Is this how you would have done it?

PETER: I'm not Sophia. I haven't suffered as she has.

VALENTINA: How has she suffered? What does she suffer? Please. I would really like to know.

PETER: Well . . .

VALENTINA: In what way is she different from anyone in Russia? What is her complaint? That she is not *free*? That's what I've been told. Well, who is free? Tell me, am I free?

SOPHIA: No. No, Mother. But it's you who always say I am docile . . . (*She turns to* PETER.) That's what she tells me. That I'm passive; I'm second-rate, I agree to things too easily . . .

VALENTINA: I say this?

SOPHIA: Today! Even today you said people take advantage of me. Now when I make a stand, you insult me.

VALENTINA: I do. Because it is doomed. Because it's not in your character.

SOPHIA: No?

VALENTINA: It's just a little spurt. You don't have the character to finish what you've started.
(*There is a pause.* SOPHIA *looks at her, as if finally understanding her objection. Then, with genuine interest:*)

SOPHIA: Is that what you fear?

VALENTINA: Yes, it is. You'll fail. You'll lose heart.

SOPHIA: Is that *all* you fear?
(VALENTINA *looks slightly shifty.*)

VALENTINA: Nor does he. I apologize for saying this. He's ten years from dying.

SOPHIA: Yes, thank you, Mother. Is there anything else?
(*She looks calmly to* PETER *who seems not remotely upset.*)

PETER: It's all right.

SOPHIA: Perhaps you might explain. I suppose my mother did not tell you anything of her own life.

PETER: Er, no.

VALENTINA: We did not discuss it.

SOPHIA: Valentina does not tell you why she's so hard on me.
(*There's a pause, the two women quite still.*)
My mother made a choice. Thirty-five years ago.

VALENTINA: Yes.

SOPHIA: I was a baby. She carried me in her arms into Russia, in 1921. She brought me here from Paris.
(*There is a pause.*)

PETER: I see.

(*He waits for more, but the two women are still, both looking down. Eventually:*)

What . . . I don't see . . . I don't understand exactly . . . I mean . . .

SOPHIA: Go on. Please. Yes. Ask.

PETER: Well . . . I suppose I'm wondering . . . do you regret it?

VALENTINA: How do you answer that question? At certain times everything is wrong.

(SOPHIA *smiles.*)

I was a wayward woman – that's the word. I lay around in beds, in studios, with men, smoking too much and thinking, shall I grow my hair? I had a child. Oh, I was like Gorki's mother, who stopped for fifteen minutes on a peasants' march to give birth in a ditch. Then she ran to catch up with the marchers. I was the same. I had my little Sophia in an atelier in the Marais, with two jugs of hot water and a homosexual friend who delivered her. And then I thought – well, is this it? This lounging about? This thinking only of yourself? This – what word should I use – *freedom*? Having a child changed everything. I suddenly decided that Paris was meaningless. Indulgence only. I had a Russian daughter. I had to come home. (*She sits back.*) An artist in Russia. Oh, when I came back, of course, everything was possible. (*She smiles.*) But now. I have not exhibited in seventeen years. (*She shrugs slightly.*) Foreign painters are exhibited in all sorts of style. But Russians may have one style only. It does not suit me. That's all there is to say.

(*There is another silence.*)

SOPHIA: My mother is intolerant of those who complain.

PETER: Yes. Do you ever think . . . you could have left here . . .

VALENTINA: Exile, you mean?

PETER: Yes.

VALENTINA: It seemed to me cowardly. To give up seems

cowardly. Finally that is always the choice. (*She gestures suddenly towards the canvas on the other side of the room.*) A painting, we are told, left by an aristocrat in his will. His last wish, to send it back to Russia. And he left in 1919! (*She laughs.*)

PETER: I don't know, I mean, for myself I've never even thought of it, why should I? But for you . . . with your background . . .

VALENTINA: No, of course not. My life is not happy. I say this to you. But it would also be unhappy if I'd been cowardly. (*She shakes her head.*) Your life is defined by an absence, by what is not happening, by where you can't be. You think all the time about 'me'. Oh 'me'! Oh 'me'! The endless 'me' who takes over. 'Me' becomes everything. Oh 'I' decided. The self-dramatization. Turning your life into a crusade. A crusade in which you claim equal status with Russia. On the one hand, the whole of Russia, millions of square miles. On the other, 'I' think and 'I' feel. The battle is unequal. That kind of self-advertisement, it seemed to me wrong. And dangerous. And wilful. To drink wine or breed horses, and dream of elsewhere. (*Pause.*) I wasn't a communist. I know what has happened since. I'm still not a communist. How could I be? But I made a decision.

PETER: And were you right?

VALENTINA: I have no idea.

(*There is a silence.*)

SOPHIA: Peter. Please. I want to be alone with her.

PETER: What? Oh, of course.

SOPHIA: Please, Peter, she and I need to talk.

PETER: Of course. (*He is upset.*) Now?

SOPHIA: Yes.

(*He stands a moment.*)

PETER: When shall I see you?

SOPHIA: What?

PETER: See you? We haven't made an arrangement.

SOPHIA: Oh no, that's right.

PETER: Well, er . . .

SOPHIA: Do we have to fix it now?

PETER: Of course we do, yes.

SOPHIA: Sorry, I can't think. You say.

PETER: In three days, do you have . . .

SOPHIA: Yes. Friday. The usual break after lunch.

PETER: Three days.

SOPHIA: Yes.

PETER: I'll see you then. And we'll talk this over. Madame Nrovka, this has been a great honour. (*He goes across to* VALENTINA.)

VALENTINA: I was pleased to meet you.

PETER: To be honest I was scared. Not because of you. But because I care too much. I do crave her happiness.

VALENTINA: Yes. That is clear.
(*He stands a moment.*)

PETER: Three days then.

SOPHIA: Yes.

PETER: I must go. (*Without looking at* SOPHIA *he turns and goes quickly out.*)

VALENTINA: Now it's cold.

SOPHIA: Yes.

VALENTINA: It's cold suddenly.

SOPHIA: They turn the heating off, I suppose.

VALENTINA: All the money they must need to heat art. To keep art warm for the public. (*She looks across at* SOPHIA.) Tell me, is it money you want?

SOPHIA: Yes, of course.

VALENTINA: I guessed that. Peter's embarrassment was on such a scale. I knew you must have told him to ask me for money.

SOPHIA: I did.

VALENTINA: He's too nice. He would have stood there for ever. (SOPHIA *smiles.*)
How much do you need?

SOPHIA: Two thousand.

VALENTINA: When?

SOPHIA: Well, after the counselling, and the advertisement, and

the examination in the Peoples' Court, finally you need the
money for the Regional Court. But I felt . . . there's no
point in my starting if at the end I can't pay.

VALENTINA: You should have asked me this morning. Before
speaking to the children. But it did not occur to you that I
would say no.

(*She looks at* SOPHIA *who does not answer.*)

Why should I give you money when I do not approve?

(*There is a silence.* SOPHIA *just looks at her.* VALENTINA *turns
away.*)

You're just unlucky. It's historical accident. In the twenties
it was easy.

SOPHIA: I've heard.

VALENTINA: In the first days of the Soviet Union, you didn't
need your partner's consent. You could sue for a divorce by
sending a postcard and three roubles. There was to be a
revolution of the sexes. I must say I had my doubts at the
time.

(SOPHIA *smiles as well.*)

I had a lover for a while. Or rather I tried to. Another
soldier. Like you, we had nowhere to go. After Paris,
Russia seemed ridiculous. Because even then, people got
upset if you showed your feelings. People disapproved. So
we noticed that at stations people may embrace openly
because they're always saying goodbye. So he and I used to
go and pretend that one of us was catching a train. We
embraced on the platform. We said a thousand goodbyes.
Train after train went without us. Then an official came and
said 'You've watched enough trains.' (*She pauses, lost in
thought.*) And what will you have? A small room in the
suburbs of Leningrad. No money. Children who dislike you
for taking them away from their father. From prosperity.
From someone who belongs. Who fits in. Who is happy
here.

SOPHIA: Yes.

VALENTINA: Have you thought of the effect the divorce will
have on him? A Party member?

SOPHIA: Of course. But if I don't I will have no self-respect.
(VALENTINA *laughs*.)

VALENTINA: Oh, please. You! No one cares. You have no status
here. Be clear. You're a private citizen. Love in a small flat,
it's nobody's business. But Grigor – he will lose position.
Influence. Friends. He will be discredited. It's a sign of
failure.
(SOPHIA *looks unapologetically at her*.)

SOPHIA: Well, I can't live with the Party any more. (*She shakes
her head*.) I've always known . . . after all, in my profession
I work with young people. I spread ideas. I can't be
considered for promotion unless I am also willing to join.
The moment is looming when they will ask me. (*She pauses
a moment*.) This way the moment will never arrive.

VALENTINA: Ah, well, I see . . .

SOPHIA: I think the only hope now is to live your life in private.

VALENTINA: So you choose Peter.

SOPHIA: Yes.

VALENTINA: Because he's ineffectual and hopeless and has no
ambition. That's clear. You love his hopelessness.

SOPHIA: It seems a great virtue. Is that wrong? After watching
Grigor. The way Grigor is. It comforts me that Peter has no
wish to get on.

VALENTINA: Yes. That's attractive. But there's a limit.

SOPHIA: You mean Peter is beyond it?

VALENTINA: He is the Soul of No Hope. (*She smiles*.) Everyone
here has a vision. How it might be other. We all have a
dream of something else. For you it's Linitsky. Linitsky's
your escape. How will it be when he becomes your reality?
When he's not your escape? When he's your life?

SOPHIA: I don't know.

VALENTINA: Have you thought . . .

SOPHIA: Of course.

VALENTINA: It's possible you'll hate him? As you hate Grigor
now.

SOPHIA: No.

VALENTINA: All the things that seem so attractive – that

43

manner, the way he holds his hat in his hands, the gentleness – when they are your life, they will seem insufferable.

SOPHIA: Perhaps. I don't know. How can anyone know?

(VALENTINA *smiles*.)

VALENTINA: Everyone here lives in the future. Or in the past. No one wants the present. What shall we do with the present? Oh, Paris! Oh, Linitsky! Anything but here! Anything but now! (*She turns to* SOPHIA.) I had a friend. She loved a violinist. They could rarely meet. He was married. She worshipped him. Eventually he could not play unless he sensed she was in the audience. She went to all his concerts for over three years. She later said to me, rather bitterly, the violin repertoire is remarkably small. The man's wife died. He came to her and said, we're free. It lasted a week. She no longer desired him. (*A pause.*) It seems to me the worst story I know.

(SOPHIA *looks at her, holding her gaze.*)

What do you feel when he says that he'll die for you? That it's life and death.

SOPHIA: Well . . .

VALENTINA: Is it for you?

(SOPHIA *pauses a moment.*)

SOPHIA: No. But we're different. I love him. I love what he is.

VALENTINA: Do you wish he loved you less desperately?

SOPHIA: That's how he loves me.

VALENTINA: And is that a good thing?

SOPHIA: Look, how can I say? He's kind to me. He'll never do me harm. I always feel I can rest with him. Yes, there is inequality. If you like, an inequality of need. Finally. But what's wrong with that? If we said, well, I can see this isn't quite perfect, we'd never do anything.

VALENTINA: No.

(*There is a pause.*)

Even so.

SOPHIA: What is the alternative? I know what you feel. But by your argument, must we put up with everything?

VALENTINA: I have.

SOPHIA: Yes. But now should I?

(VALENTINA *turns and looks at her, but does not answer.*)

Mother, will you give me the money?

VALENTINA: Of course. (*She laughs.*) Mind you, I don't have it.

SOPHIA: What?

VALENTINA: Two thousand roubles, are you joking?

SOPHIA: I assumed . . .

VALENTINA: Oh yes, I act as if I'm rich. That seems to me simply good manners. Don't you see through it?

SOPHIA: No.

VALENTINA: Look at my life. How do you think I would have that kind of money?

(SOPHIA *begins to laugh.*)

SOPHIA: I thought you were frugal.

VALENTINA: Frugal? I'm poor.

SOPHIA: Oh Lord, no, I don't believe it. I've been so nervous . . .

VALENTINA: Well, so you should be. But not about money. You mustn't worry. I'll sell my flat.

SOPHIA: Don't be ridiculous.

VALENTINA: Yes. It means nothing. Goodness, if I couldn't throw money away I'd really be tragic.

SOPHIA: No, there's no question . . .

VALENTINA: Yes. I shall do it. To shame you.

SOPHIA: Well, we shall see. (*A pause.*) You'll support me? You think I'm doing right?

VALENTINA: There is no right. Until you see that, you will never have peace. (*She gets up. She walks right the way across the room, decisively.*) I will speak to Grigor. No, not for you. Not to help you. But on behalf of the children, I will persuade him not to oppose you, so that it's quicker in the Regional Court. He's frightened of women. Most bullies are.

(SOPHIA *is about to speak but* VALENTINA *interrupts quickly.*)

Don't ask me any more. That's all I can do. Now please go. The man you want to live with is senile. Senile's the word.

SOPHIA: Thank you, Mother.

VALENTINA: You won't be happy. You'll die at forty.

SOPHIA: Good. Well, I'm glad that you're pleased.

(*She smiles, genuinely moved.*)

VALENTINA: I'm not pleased.

SOPHIA: Come here.

VALENTINA: No.

SOPHIA: Mother, please. Embrace me.

VALENTINA: Don't be stupid.

(SOPHIA *is holding out her arms.* VALENTINA *doesn't move. So* SOPHIA *moves across and embraces her. Then she holds her head in her hands.*)

SOPHIA: Hey, Mother, hey.

(VALENTINA *is about to cry.* SOPHIA *stops her.*)

VALENTINA: You must go. Give my love to the children. Tell them to visit me.

SOPHIA: Yes.

VALENTINA: Whatever you do, this time you must live with it.

SOPHIA: Yes. I've learnt that from you.

(*She looks at her a moment. Then she turns and goes out. There's a moment's silence. Then* VALENTINA *walks across to the chair and picks up the canvas from the leg against which it is propped. She holds it out at arms' length for five seconds. Then, without any visible reaction, she puts it down. Then she walks across the room and stands alone. Then her eyes begin to fill with tears. Silently the* ASSISTANT CURATOR *returns, standing respectfully at the door.*)

VALENTINA: You've come back.

ASSISTANT: Yes.

VALENTINA: I didn't hear you.

ASSISTANT: Have you had time to look at it?

VALENTINA: I've examined it.

(*There's a pause.*)

Yes. It's Matisse.

(*Neither of them moves.*)

Not, surely, the beginning of a sequence.

ASSISTANT: I'm sorry?

VALENTINA: No, it's just . . . you said . . . there was nothing in
the foreground, so you assumed this is where he started.
Then later he put in the woman. Or the violin. But no. It
was the opposite. He removed the woman. He sought to
distil.

ASSISTANT: Oh, I see. Yes. That fits with the scientific dating.

VALENTINA: Yes, it would. You could have saved yourself
money.

(*The* ASSISTANT *stands a moment, puzzled by her tone.*)

ASSISTANT: Do you need to take another look?

VALENTINA: No. He said that finally he didn't need a model.
Finally he didn't even need paint. *He* was there. He was a
person. Present. And that was enough.

(*The* ASSISTANT *moves, as if to pick the canvas up.*)

The giveaway is the light through the shutters. No one else
could do that. The way the sun is diffused. He controlled
the sun in his painting. He said, with shutters he could
summon the sun as surely as Joshua with his trumpet.

ASSISTANT: Yes. I see what you mean.

(*She turns and looks at him.*)

VALENTINA: And are you a Member?

ASSISTANT: What?

VALENTINA: The Party. Do you belong?

ASSISTANT: Oh.

VALENTINA: No. Don't tell me. I know. As surely as if you
were a painting. (*She holds a hand up towards him, as if
judging him. Then smiles.*) Yes. You belong.

ASSISTANT: In my job you have to. I mean, I want to, as well. If
I want advancement. This painting is going to be a great
help to me.

VALENTINA: So Matisse did not paint in vain. (*She gathers up
her coat.*) I must go. (*Before she is ready, she turns
thoughtfully a moment.*) He was once in a Post Office in
Picardy. He was waiting to pick up the phone. He picked
up a telegraph form lying on the table, and without
thinking, began to draw a woman's head. All the time he
talked on the phone, he was drawing. And when at the end,

47

he looked down, he had drawn his mother's face. His hand did the work, not the brain. And he said the result was truer and more beautiful than anything that came as an effort of will.

(*She stands a moment, then turns to go.*)

ASSISTANT: I'll get you a car.

VALENTINA: No. The tram is outside. It goes right by my door.

(*She goes. He stands a moment, looking at the painting. The background fades and the stage is filled with the image of the bay at Nice: a pair of open French windows, a balcony, the sea and the sky.*

The ASSISTANT *turns and looks to the open door.*)

WRECKED EGGS

CHARACTERS

GRACE
ROBBIE
LOELIA

The cast for *Wrecked Eggs* was as follows:

GRACE	Zoë Wanamaker
ROBBIE	Colin Stinton
LOELIA	Kate Buffery
Design	John Gunter
Lighting	Rory Dempster
Director	David Hare

The scene is set in Rhinebeck, New York State, in the present day.

The living room of a clapboard house in upstate New York, by the
Hudson. A pleasant wooden living room is sparsely furnished with
comfortable, unpretentious country things. Outside the light and heat
are fierce, but the slatted blinds are so dark that inside it seems cool.
At the back, a door with a fly-screen gives on to the garden. At the
side another door leads through to the stairs and the kitchen. On the
gramophone Nat King Cole is just coming to the end of 'Nature
Boy'. GRACE *is sitting on the sofa listening to* ROBBIE. *They are*
both in their thirties. He wears a check shirt and pressed slacks. He
has an easy, slightly serious manner. GRACE *is auburn-haired, with*
a light humorous voice, and a charming air of amusement.

GRACE: How did he die?

ROBBIE: He died going to the laundry. He walked straight out
into the street with his laundry bag. The driver didn't see
him.

GRACE: Oh God, that's terrible.
(*There is a pause.*)

ROBBIE: Would you like a steak?

GRACE: No, thank you.

ROBBIE: I lit the barbecue.

GRACE: No, that's very kind.
(*Neither of them move.*)
What about his wife?

ROBBIE: His wife was shattered. She didn't know.

GRACE: What?

ROBBIE: Pardon me?

GRACE: What didn't she know?

ROBBIE: That he had another wife.

GRACE: Ah.

ROBBIE: She didn't know he was a bigamist. Until he was run
over. That's how she found out.

GRACE: I see. (*She hesitates a moment, puzzled.*) But you said . . .
he just had a laundry bag . . .

53

ROBBIE: Yeah. He had two apartments. This was outside the other one.

GRACE: How had he done that?

ROBBIE: Oh well, the second wife wanted a green card. She was Malaysian.

GRACE: Don't they look you up?

ROBBIE: When?

GRACE: When you do that? When you ask to marry someone? Don't they check you out to see if by chance you're already married?

ROBBIE: I don't know. They just had a lot of Fingerhuts, I guess.

GRACE: It's not a common name.

ROBBIE: I don't know how he did it. I only know he had a girl in the West Seventies who came from Malaysia and was his second wife. And he had another in the East Sixties. And she was a Boston brahmin, and she never crossed the park. (*Through the hall door comes* LOELIA. *She is slightly younger than the others, early rather than mid-thirties. Tall and thin, with fine thick hair, she wears tennis shorts, rolled-down white socks and a T-shirt. She radiates good health.*)

I was telling Grace about Dexter.

LOELIA: Dexter with two wives?

ROBBIE: Yeah.

LOELIA: He's attained the status of myth with Robert.

ROBBIE: No, not entirely.

LOELIA: It's what Robert wants.

ROBBIE: No . . . (*He smiles.*) What I want is a woman who'll surprise me.

LOELIA: Oh, yes?

ROBBIE: Who won't tell me when she's going to come over. She'll just ring the bell. On an evening when I'm not expecting her. And then when she goes she won't tell me when she's coming again.

(LOELIA *is standing behind the sofa. She speaks quietly, neutrally.*)

LOELIA: He's a boy.

GRACE: I can see.

LOELIA: The first few weeks you know him it's charming.

ROBBIE: You still like it. (*He smiles at her. Turns to* GRACE.) So what about you?

GRACE: What?

ROBBIE: Are you getting married?

GRACE: What you mean, just once?

ROBBIE: Well, I assume.

(GRACE *looks down. Decisively:*)

GRACE: No.

(GRACE *looks across at* LOELIA.)

ROBBIE: It's just Loelia said . . .

LOELIA: (*Embarrassed*) Robbie . . .

ROBBIE: That you were . . .

GRACE: Yes. I was. But I got rid of it. I had to. I feel . . . oh Lord, I mean . . . I have the most extraordinary gift for getting pregnant. It's hopeless. I don't know what to do. I've been fitted for a diaphragm. I only fuck on certain days of my cycle. Always afterward I send in the spermicide squad.

ROBBIE: Squad?

GRACE: From a tube.

ROBBIE: Oh, I see.

GRACE: But it doesn't do the job. I am ridiculously fertile. My greenhouse is permanently at 100 degrees.

LOELIA: Me too.

GRACE: I feel so strange about infertile people. I keep hearing of couples . . . you know . . . whose whole life is trying. But I can't stop. (*She pauses decisively.*)

ROBBIE: Have you ended one before?

GRACE: Yes.

ROBBIE: So's Loelia.

LOELIA: Yes. A couple of times.

GRACE: I've done it . . . oh, too often. I swore I'd never do it again.

(LOELIA *is watching her.*)

I mean I'm going to have to take the pill again. Which gives you cancer. So either I give up sex, or I have sex and

55

cancer. It's nothing or both. You can't just choose one.

ROBBIE: Don't they have these new low-level pills?

(LOELIA *speaks forcefully, but, as ever, without bitterness or sarcasm.*)

LOELIA: Only a man could ask in that tone of fatuous optimism. Yes. But you sprout hair. Or you get lumps. Or you feel dizzy when you go for a walk.

GRACE: Or you get pregnant.

LOELIA: None of them work. Nothing works. Except abstinence. Which is out of the question. (*There is a pause.*) Sex is the one thing which never lets you down. (*She thinks a moment. It is suddenly very quiet.*)

ROBBIE: No, that's right. Do people want a drink?

GRACE: Somerset Maugham said that half his schoolfriends had devoted themselves to career, and half to seducing women. And at sixty the ones who had spent their lives chasing women did not seem noticeably deprived of happiness.

ROBBIE: No. No. Well, I'm sure. (*There's a pause. The women are still, but* ROBBIE *seems uneasy.*) But of course if you're a lawyer . . .

GRACE: Sorry?

ROBBIE: What . . . no, I mean, I'm too busy . . .

LOELIA: Robbie has to run to stand still. He has no time to look at other women.

ROBBIE: That's right. (*He shakes his head.*) No, it's tricky. My nut is one hundred thousand dollars.

GRACE: Gee whiz.

LOELIA: He's got the biggest nut on the block.

ROBBIE: That's what I need every year just to maintain our apartment and . . . I really have to work pretty hard, Loelia has to work . . .

LOELIA: I do.

ROBBIE: We both have to work, just to live in Manhattan, keep this place. I'm at the office most evenings. Preparing a brief. Just to hit that nut.

LOELIA: That's before he even gets on to pleasure. Pleasure's extra for Robbie.

ROBBIE: That's right. So I guess . . . (*He smiles, expansive.*) I've no time for fooling around.

LOELIA: He likes me because I'm here and I'm quick.

ROBBIE: That's not quite true, Loelia.

LOELIA: I barely interrupt his work. The effect of finding someone else would impede his working pattern.

ROBBIE: (*Firmer*) Loelia, I think we both wanted this style of life.

(*There is a pause.*)

What's your nut?

GRACE: What? Oh. Do I have one? I suppose I must.

ROBBIE: Your monthly outgoing? Just to stand still?

GRACE: Do you know . . . I have no idea. (*She smiles, as if thinking it over.*) I'm in a cash business, it's all entertaining . . .

ROBBIE: Ah well.

GRACE: Little bits of money in tin cans. I find dimes in my shoes and dollars in between the pages of the books I'm reading.

ROBBIE: Well, that's good. I'm surprised you have time to read.

GRACE: I don't have time to read. But I don't do my job. My job disgusts me. So I sit and read a book instead.

ROBBIE: Oh really? Wow. (*He frowns.*) I thought you had a good job.

GRACE: It is a good job. It leaves me time to read novels.

ROBBIE: Oh yeah, well, that's a good job. I suppose. (*He seems upset by this.*)

GRACE: If people say, why am I not in the paper, I say, well I tried but they wouldn't let you in.

ROBBIE: No. (*He reaches for a copy of the* New York Times *behind him.*) How *do* they decide?

GRACE: How?

ROBBIE: What to put in the paper? I mean, look at this . . . (*He points to a lead story, then to another way down the page.*) Why is that there? And not that?

GRACE: Oh well, mostly it's to do with success.

ROBBIE: What do you mean?

GRACE: Reading about success is the new pornography. Look, I'll show you. (*She goes to search in a soft bag which she has left, unpacked, near the door. From it she eventually removes a file.*) I keep this as a warning. If we had censors in this country and their job was to cut every article which uses the word 'survivor', if they cut every word about *success*, if they cut every word about the rich and their apartments, and what they eat, and what they sit on, and what they have on their walls, and where they go in the summer, and what other rich people they're sharing beds with, and why we should envy them, and why we should think they are wonderful people really, or in spite of it, or because of it, and how exactly they made it, and why they made it and other people didn't, and what incredible pressure they have to put up with, and what a bore it is to be recognized, and how difficult it is once you're successful to go on being successful, if we cut every article which implies what's successful must be good, if we just said sorry – press censorship – this is Russia – none of that may appear . . . (*From the file she removes a copy of the* Times.) Then this is the form in which you would get your average morning paper. (*She holds it up. It is like a conjuror's paper trick. So much has been cut from it that it barely hangs together. It is just latticed shreds.*)

LOELIA: My God, look at it.

(GRACE *holds her hand up.*)

GRACE: And now I shall read a copy of an average best-selling weekly magazine. (*She reaches into the bag. She moves towards the centre of the room. She has nothing in her hands. She mimes reading a non-existent magazine.*)

ROBBIE: Oh, I get it. It's nothing.

GRACE: And once you know that's what it is, once you stop reading anything, *anything* which invites you to envy success, then you will find your daily reading material reduced to the back of cornflake boxes. (*She smiles and throws the shredded paper aside.*)

LOELIA: I read Robbie's rubbers.

GRACE: What?

ROBBIE: What did you say?

LOELIA: No, I just . . . taking up . . . no, you reminded me
. . . the best thing to read in this country, you said . . . I
was reading the pack. You were asleep.

GRACE: What did it say?

LOELIA: It was very strange. I meant to remark on it. It said
they had a five-year guarantee.

ROBBIE: (*Puzzled*) Well?

LOELIA: What puzzles me is, there are only six in the pack.

GRACE: (*Getting it*) Oh yes, very good.

LOELIA: I mean, what sort of life are they expecting us to lead?
What sort of person makes a pack last over five years? What
are they, rubbers for abstinents?

GRACE: Monks' rubbers.

LOELIA: They should sell it. That's a good name.

(GRACE *laughs and sits down.*)

ROBBIE: Now look . . .

LOELIA: There's no need to get angry.

ROBBIE: I'm not getting angry, OK? It makes sense what
they're saying. They're saying 'You may keep these for five
years.' Not 'You may use these over a five-year period.'
That would be asinine.

LOELIA: It would be superhuman.

ROBBIE: It's a perfectly sensible offer. From a responsible firm.
To whom we have cause to be grateful. You say nothing
works. Well, rubbers work.

(*There is a difficult silence. He seems disproportionately
emphatic.*)

LOELIA: They are not aphrodisiac.

ROBBIE: No. That is one of their faults. But they are effective.

(*A pause. He still seems annoyed.*)

GRACE: The Romans used half an orange.

ROBBIE: Oh really?

GRACE: Yes. They scooped it out first.

ROBBIE: Yeah, well, I'd pictured that. When you said it, I
visualized it peel only. Hemi-spherical.

GRACE: Often I've felt it's destiny. Nothing can stop me having kids.

(*She is looking at* LOELIA *who nods slightly, understanding.*)

ROBBIE: Who . . . (*He stops.*)

GRACE: What?

ROBBIE: No, I wondered who the father was.

LOELIA: Robbie . . .

GRACE: No, it's fine. He's a guy . . . I don't see him now.

ROBBIE: Oh.

GRACE: I met him through work. He . . . oh, we had a lot of shouting and screaming. He always said he wanted to live with me. But the moment he moved in . . . well, it seemed to bring out the Japanese army in him.

LOELIA: You mean it got rough?

GRACE: Suddenly. (*She stops, thinking about it.*) It's odd.

ROBBIE: I don't understand the Japanese.

GRACE: I'm sorry?

ROBBIE: I'll tell you, I read . . . there was this Captain. On a container ship. A couple of Toyotas fell off into the sea. He feels he's responsible. So he kills himself. (*He shakes his head.*) I mean, I don't understand this behaviour. It puzzles me.

GRACE: No.

ROBBIE: It seems excessive. It seems *foreign*.

GRACE: Mmm.

LOELIA: At the very least.

GRACE: And it's hell to deal with them. They think saying no to people is rude. That means if you have to do business, there's three days of saying yes all the time. Then finally the fourth they will say, er there is a slight problem. You see, they think it's impolite to disagree. (*She smiles.*) That can make life pretty laborious.

LOELIA: The ones I don't get are the ones who are so desperate to die.

ROBBIE: Right. Oh, sure.

LOELIA: When Hirohito surrendered . . . I've seen this newsreel. All these Japanese soldiers at the end of the war, and they're all weeping and wailing and falling on each others' necks, and just gushing, because they're not going to have their chance to get killed.

ROBBIE: No, that is eerie.

LOELIA: It's weird.

GRACE: It's peculiar.

(*There is a pause.*)

ROBBIE: I've heard they've started sleeping in tubes.

LOELIA: What?

ROBBIE: I read there's so little space now in the cities that when they build a hotel, the rooms are just cylinders. With beds in. You crawl in.

GRACE: I've heard that.

ROBBIE: And also – another thing – in Japan you don't have a bath. You have a bath *before* you have a bath. So you're clean before you get in.

LOELIA: What's the point of that?

ROBBIE: It's purer. The bath is purer. You don't dirty it.

(*There's a pause, while they all think about this.*)

Well, now you'll be able to go.

(GRACE *looks up. She doesn't understand this last remark.*)

LOELIA: What?

ROBBIE: No, you're always saying you don't go anywhere. Now you'll be able to. You can go to Japan.

(GRACE *frowns, puzzled.*)

GRACE: I'm sorry. I don't understand you. About Loelia.

ROBBIE: Oh I see, no. I didn't mention. Loelia and I are going to split up.

(ROBBIE *is smiling at* GRACE. LOELIA *is still. Only* GRACE *seems put out.*)

GRACE: I'm sorry.

ROBBIE: No, it's fine.

GRACE: Ah. Really?

ROBBIE: I mean, I don't mean, I mean obviously . . . it's painful. Of course. But Loelia and I are both adults. We've talked it over.

(*He takes a sidelong glance at* LOELIA, *who is watching* GRACE.)

GRACE: I should never have come.

ROBBIE: Why?

GRACE: Oh God, I feel awful. When you were . . .

ROBBIE: No, we welcomed it.

GRACE: Oh good.

LOELIA: Robbie had this idea.

(*She says this a little coolly.* GRACE *catches the tone and looks at her.*)

ROBBIE: I wanted to celebrate.

GRACE: Celebrate?

ROBBIE: Oh, I don't mean the fact of it.

GRACE: Isn't that a little unusual?

ROBBIE: I always think in this country we don't know how to perform rites of passage. We don't know how to mark them.

GRACE: Huh.

ROBBIE: We're very bad. All the important moments. Birth. Marriage. Death, obviously. In other cultures, people know how to handle them. They have rituals. I mean, look at the people in India.

GRACE: What do they do?

ROBBIE: They put their family on pyres by the Ganges. And then set light to them. I tell you, I had a friend once. His father died. He said he found the whole business surprisingly liberating. Just to build the fire. To wait. To sit there while your father's body goes up. Just to observe the ritual. This feeling that there's a form in which things should be done. This is the formula. This is the observance.

(*There is a pause.*)

LOELIA: I've bought an apartment. I move in on Monday.

ROBBIE: And so I was thinking – to mark this – let's have a weekend.

GRACE: Uh-huh.

ROBBIE: I mean, it's odd, we barely know you . . .

GRACE: No.

ROBBIE: In fact you and I hadn't met . . .

GRACE: I only met Loelia last week.

LOELIA: That's it.

GRACE: I needed some work on my backhand.

ROBBIE: But the times Loelia and I have been happiest – well, *some* of the best times have been when we've had a few people round.

GRACE: Mmm.

ROBBIE: Drunk beer. Cooked dinner. Hung out. I thought it would be nice to do it as a final ritual.

GRACE: Yes. (*She frowns a moment.*) Is anyone else coming?

ROBBIE: We asked a whole stack of people. Old friends. I think we were too vague. We said, just come if you're free. Drop by. Let's not formalize it. Let's say, you're welcome. Don't be embarrassed. Don't be depressed. We're here. We're coping. (*He seems lost a moment. Then he smiles.*) We're planning to serve a large meal.

GRACE: Oh good.

ROBBIE: As a final . . . (*He gestures.*) I've got a barbecue.

LOELIA: What?

ROBBIE: I lit the barbecue.

LOELIA: Robbie, I've got a whole thing in the kitchen.

ROBBIE: What d'you mean?

LOELIA: Linguine. I've got soft-shell crabs marinating. And I've got veal. I'm making my blanquette.

ROBBIE: (*Laughs*) Oh no, I don't believe it. I went to the market this morning. While you were having a game. I got steaks. And Italian sausages. I was going to make cornbread.

LOELIA: I can't believe it.

ROBBIE: No, well it's true.

(*They are both laughing, delighted.*)

LOELIA: That's wonderful.

ROBBIE: Two dinners.

GRACE: An excess of hospitality. An absence of guests.

ROBBIE: Loelia's a really outstanding cook. (*He is shaking his head, beaming at her.*)

LOELIA: I went to the New School croissant and brioche class. It costs forty dollars, but you get to keep what you make.

ROBBIE: Boy, that was good. She used to come back to the apartment on a Saturday morning with what she'd just made. She did one which nearly made me faint. With cinnamon and raisins.

LOELIA: I did.

ROBBIE: She also did a plain one.

LOELIA: That was the best. The best was classic.

ROBBIE: Yeah. It was great.

(*They are looking at each other so fondly that* GRACE *is a little embarrassed*.)

GRACE: Is your cooking good?

ROBBIE: Oh yeah, mine's good too. Not in Loelia's class.

LOELIA: He cooks like an angel. He does a cajun stew with gulf prawns and okra that breaks my heart every time I eat it.

ROBBIE: I serve it really thick.

LOELIA: He made it the night he proposed to me. That's how I knew he was going to be the right man for me.

(*They smile*.)

GRACE: That's nice.

ROBBIE: We had been lent a house on the beach at Cape Cod. It was an A-frame. One side of it was glass. With a wooden balcony. You could walk straight down to the ocean.

LOELIA: I didn't have a chance.

ROBBIE: No, that's right.

(*There is a pause*.)

She was mine for the taking.

(LOELIA *smiles*.)

She had no experience with gentlemen. That's how I did it. With manners. Loelia told me nobody had ever thought to propose to her before.

LOELIA: It wasn't quite true.

ROBBIE: It was a lie, you mean?

LOELIA: No. Of course not. It's just . . . I didn't tell you everything. Always. I had to be careful. (*She turns to* GRACE *and smiles*.) I was being thoughtful. He hated my past.

ROBBIE: Loelia was a hippy.

LOELIA: No, I wasn't. Only by your standards.

ROBBIE: There was a photo . . .

LOELIA: Oh, come on.

ROBBIE: May I say this?

LOELIA: Go ahead.

ROBBIE: She had her photo in a magazine. As she bathed in a pond at a rock concert. She had no clothes on.

GRACE: Before you knew her?

LOELIA: Yes. It was muddy. I came out dirtier than when I got in.

ROBBIE: I guess I was shocked. At the time. I remember I hated it.

LOELIA: Not as much as your parents did.

GRACE: How did they see it?

LOELIA: It was in our apartment.

GRACE: What did they say?

ROBBIE: Oh well, nothing. My mother was OK.

LOELIA: It was your father.

(*She looks away a moment. There is a pause.* ROBBIE *looks down.*)

ROBBIE: He's an odd man. (*Then he smiles.*) We used to go up to the sand-dunes. Do you know them?

GRACE: Mmm.

ROBBIE: By Provincetown. Loelia at that time was just starting out.

LOELIA: I had no money. It never occurred to me there could be a profession called tennis coach. Up till then I'd been trying to work in offices.

GRACE: Yes. I still do.

LOELIA: I hated it. It seemed unhealthy. I hated the artificial light. You get worked up about things that don't matter. They *seem* to matter. They become your whole world. For the time you're in there. Then when you walk away it's like . . . who's that man in high school philosophy who says it's not there when you're not looking?

ROBBIE: Bishop Berkeley.

LOELIA: Him.

GRACE: Oh, but it is. It is there. It does matter.

ROBBIE: (*Frowns*) What makes you say that?

(GRACE *looks at him a moment.*)

GRACE: No, I don't know, I think it's too easy, that sort of attitude. I mean, I have it, I have it at work. I just walk away from things. I've spent my life walking away from things. Which I can see is a luxury. It's only a certain kind of person who can do that.

ROBBIE: What kind?

GRACE: A person . . . with a good income, for a start. (*She smiles.*) It's something I dislike in myself. The right to withdraw. To think myself superior. For instance, the office I now work in is full of . . . I don't know . . . ridiculous people, the job I do is absurd . . .

ROBBIE: I'm sure that's not true.

GRACE: And yet I collect a salary. I eat. I prosper. I decorate the office. With my nice skirts. And my smile. And because I'm reasonably smart and one step ahead, although I disdain what I'm doing, I don't get fired.

ROBBIE: I bet you're good at it.

GRACE: Oh sure, I make the calls. The phone is jammed to my ear all day. I call a few people. 'Hey, Grace, will you call a few people? We've got a client – needs his image re-spraying.' And off I go.

(ROBBIE *is already shaking his head.*)

ROBBIE: This is a ridiculous argument. You mean, because you think what you do is silly, it's immoral to pick up your money? Are you crazy? Do you know how many people would like to pick up your money for you? Do you know how hard it is to make money at all? (*He is indignant.*) And you're worried about your *attitude*?

GRACE: I wonder, did you mention a beer?

ROBBIE: Of course.

LOELIA: Will you get it?

(ROBBIE *has already got up to go out to the kitchen.* GRACE *now gets up and walks to the other side of the room.*)

GRACE: Yes, no, I can see it seems silly . . .

ROBBIE: (*Calling from the kitchen*) It's wacky, for God's sake. What do you think jobs are like?

(LOELIA *is sitting in her chair, watching* GRACE. *She speaks quietly, so* ROBBIE *doesn't hear.*)

LOELIA: Ignore him.

GRACE: I'm sorry?

LOELIA: He likes to talk.

(GRACE *frowns slightly at* LOELIA, *as* ROBBIE *goes on calling through.*)

ROBBIE: (*Kitchen*) Nobody's job is satisfying. It can't be. All the time. You work to make money. If you make money, your job is a success. It's as simple as that.

GRACE: (*Smiles*) Does he feel this?

LOELIA: Yes. It's a creed.

(ROBBIE *returns, handing a can of beer to* GRACE *who is now standing by the window.*)

ROBBIE: And when you make money then your job begins to seem interesting – there you are –

GRACE: Thank you.

ROBBIE: It's a two-way thing. Not every job can be interesting. It's impossible. There's a lot of shitty work. What's nice about money is when you get it, it speaks to you. It says 'What you do is shitty: now here's a reward.' Money doesn't bullshit, that's what's so good about it, money is . . . well, the great thing is . . . money is *straight*.

GRACE: I see. Well.

LOELIA: (*Smiles*) Is it manly?

ROBBIE: Money? Sure money's manly. No question. I like it. It's there. We all understand it. It's universally accepted. You know what you've got. You want something? Right, then pay for it. (*He looks down a moment.*) Money's good because it puts a value on things.

(*There is a pause.*)

GRACE: Well, goodness.

LOELIA: I know.

GRACE: And is money everything?

ROBBIE: Well, no, obviously because . . . here we are in Rhinebeck . . .

(*He gestures to the outside.* GRACE *is puzzled.*)

GRACE: I'm sorry. I can't follow . . .

ROBBIE: I mean, there's quality of life. What we have here. At weekends. By the Hudson. Paid for, I admit, by money.

GRACE: Most certainly.

ROBBIE: Quality of life is something else. It's to do with good taste. And judgement. And there's relationships.

GRACE: Yes. Are they to do with money as well?

(ROBBIE *looks across to* LOELIA. *He seems embarrassed.*)

ROBBIE: I couldn't say. What do you think?

GRACE: I could afford my abortion. (*At once she looks away.*) I'm sorry. I shouldn't have said that. It was crude. (*She pauses.*) To be honest . . . I haven't got over it. That's why . . . you must forgive me . . . that's why I accepted to come. It was selfish. I needed to get away this weekend.

(*There is a pause.*)

It takes it out of you. These visits to the clinic. You hear all these things people say about it being too easy. They must be mad. How can it ever be easy? It takes its toll. Whatever happens. However carefully you go into it. Moralists, religionists don't seem to realize: there is always a price. There's damage.

(*There is a pause. She's quiet.*)

Only a fool would say it's easy.

ROBBIE: Yes. I can see.

GRACE: (*Smiles*) And it's worse because the father is so young. He's twenty-three. He's just a boy. In jeans. Who I like very much. And he liked me. Who now is furious because . . . (*She stops.*) I don't know why I'm saying this.

ROBBIE: Please go on.

GRACE: No, I can't.

LOELIA: Please.

ROBBIE: This is in confidence. We won't tell anyone. No one else seems to be coming. To our ritual. Eh, Loelia?

LOELIA: (*Smiles*) No.

(*There is a pause.*)

GRACE: He's furious because he wanted to hold on to the child. (*At once she turns away.*) There, oh shit, I shouldn't have said it.

68

ROBBIE: It's fine.

GRACE: He's twenty-three. It's not remotely realistic. I would have ended up being the one . . .

ROBBIE: Sure you would.

GRACE: Who had to do everything.

LOELIA: Yes.

GRACE: He had no idea! He said he wanted it. He said he was up for what it involved. But what does that mean? Equal time, looking after the baby? You're joking. And I thought, do I really want a relationship that, in some form or other, will now have to last for the rest of my life? Because whatever you do, that's what it means. This way it's over.

ROBBIE: Is it over?

GRACE: He's staking out my apartment. That's why . . . when Loelia asked, it was convenient. (*A slight pause. Quietly:*) I've been sleeping at a friend's. I'm scared to go home.

(ROBBIE *looks to* LOELIA *a moment.*)

ROBBIE: Who is the boy?

GRACE: He's the son of a client.

ROBBIE: Is he an actor?

GRACE: What makes you say that?

ROBBIE: I thought you did actors.

GRACE: No. Not specifically. I do everyone. (*She smiles.*) I'm anyone's.

(ROBBIE *smiles too.* GRACE *quietly:*)

Everyone wants a press agent these days.

(*There is a companionable silence.*)

ROBBIE: Yes.

GRACE: In fact I don't like doing actors. They're so dependent on praise. Actors of forty or fifty and you still have to say 'I thought you were great.' It's so undignified. The man on the corner doesn't expect it. When you buy a paper, you don't have to say 'This is a really great newspaper stand.' Why do we have to do it for actors?

LOELIA: People need praise.

GRACE: Oh really?

LOELIA: Yes.

(GRACE *looks between them a moment.*)

GRACE: Do you praise Loelia?

ROBBIE: No, but we're married. We've been married a long
time. Being here . . . wanting her . . . that's the way I
praise her. I praise her by needing her.

(*He smiles. There is a pause.* GRACE *spreads her arms.*)

GRACE: I have no idea why you're planning to split up.

ROBBIE: Well . . .

GRACE: You seem to me to be ideally in love. Jesus, how long
have you been together?

LOELIA: Ten years.

GRACE: I mean, ten years and you're smiling and laughing, and
having a good time. And cooking two dinners. Neither of
them eggs.

LOELIA: (*Smiles*) What d'you mean?

GRACE: With me, it's eggs always. I say to myself, 'How do you
want 'em? Fried, boiled or wrecked?' 'Oh hell, just wreck
'em,' I say. (*She smiles.*) With you it's real dinners.
Doubled. How I envy this . . . ease that you have. You
have this nice home. You have flowers. You have trees.
And in some way, I can tell, it's all *real* to you.

ROBBIE: Real to us?

GRACE: Yes. It comforts you.

(*There is a pause.* ROBBIE *frowns.*)

ROBBIE: Why yes, it does.

GRACE: That's right. And I can't get that comfort. You know,
you come in here, you look at these *things* – that bookshelf,
that record player, this sofa, you think, right, these are
people to whom the comforts of life are actually real. (*She
gestures round the room.*) And I envy that . . .

LOELIA: I see.

GRACE: Because I don't have it.

LOELIA: Do you live in a mess?

GRACE: I do rather. Yes. But it's not just the mess. I'm a
heretic. I don't want a pick-up truck. Or a satellite dish on
the side of the house.

(ROBBIE *is interrupting, puzzled.*)

ROBBIE: But 'things' are surely . . . in a way they're what you work for. Shit, I'm working five days a week. Most evenings I'm working. Even these weekends – which are meant to be what I work *for* – I'm bringing back work with me. (*He points to a great pile of files and legal textbooks on one side of the room.*) Look, it's over there. (*He frowns.*) I don't see what's wrong with that.

GRACE: No, it's not right or wrong. It's a question of temperament. And no question, I envy yours. (*She smiles and looks out of the window. A moment's calm.*) Look out here. The pool is so beautiful. Who'll get the house?

ROBBIE: Oh. When we split?

GRACE: Yes.

ROBBIE: We're talking time-share. Loelia and I are staying good friends.

GRACE: Oh well, that's nice.

ROBBIE: Yeah. We're keeping it civilized.

GRACE: Civilized's good.

ROBBIE: Yeah.

GRACE: I prefer civilized.

ROBBIE: It's also better for Danny.

GRACE: Danny?

LOELIA: Our son.

GRACE: Oh I see. (*She frowns slightly.*) Where's he?

LOELIA: He's at camp.

ROBBIE: Little tyke. (*He grins at the thought of Danny.*) We don't see why just because you break up with someone, you have to be enemies for life.
(*He smiles at* LOELIA. *There is a pause.*)

GRACE: No.

LOELIA: In fact it's weird, I still know most of my exs . . . sorry, Robbie . . .

ROBBIE: No, it's OK.

LOELIA: I'm on terms with them. Ex-lovers. (*She giggles.*) Not husbands. I've only had one.

GRACE: Unlike Fingerhut.

ROBBIE: Fingerhut. Yeah. What d'you think? Do you think *his* home was full of objects?

GRACE: Well, I'd guess one was. The one in the East Sixties.

ROBBIE: Yeah. (*He's seductive, enjoying the game.*) And the West? On the West Side?

GRACE: Oh, I guess, in the other, they fucked on the floor. (*They all smile.*)

And of course he *always* ate two dinners . . .

ROBBIE: Oh yeah, he'd be at home with us.

LOELIA: If he weren't lying squashed in the road. (*She laughs. She is becoming light-headed.*) No, I saw one . . .

ROBBIE: What?

LOELIA: Ex-lover. I'm talking exs.
(*He looks pained, so she stops.*)
Robbie, I'm sorry, I'll shut up.

ROBBIE: No, it's just . . . in two days you can talk all you like. Next week when I'm gone you can talk about anything.

LOELIA: Yeah, but it won't be such fun.
(GRACE *grins.*)
It'll be strange not to have a relationship. Sometimes I think, all the attention you have to give it, it's like watering some plant every day. I was reading about the Crusades, all I could think was: these medieval knights, they left their wives for twelve years. They seemed to have no sense of how to *work* at a relationship.

ROBBIE: Loelia . . .

LOELIA: Think of all the nuances they missed. 'Oh God, did I upset you? I was gone fifteen years. Was that very hard for you?' (*She roars with laughter.*) I just love it.

ROBBIE: Yes, we can see. (*He looks to* GRACE, *a little embarrassed.*) That's what it was . . . it's what I like about Loelia. She has a sense of humour.

LOELIA: I do.

ROBBIE: I like that. The first time I met her . . .

LOELIA: Oh, Robbie . . .

ROBBIE: No, oh God, it still makes me laugh.

GRACE: What happened?

ROBBIE: No, I was . . . it's a silly story.

(*They are smiling at each other.*)

GRACE: Go on.

LOELIA: I'd written to his father because I was a student and I'd just heard about his case . . .

GRACE: I'm lost. His case?

ROBBIE: That part doesn't matter. She was a student. She was really in trouble. Just picture her. Hair out to here . . . (*He gestures.*)

LOELIA: I'd never grown up. I was a child.

ROBBIE: She still slept with a finger in her mouth.

LOELIA: Yeah. And it wasn't always my own.

(*She laughs.* ROBBIE *is also getting very excited.*)

ROBBIE: She was *really* . . .

LOELIA: I had no kind of *discipline*. Jesus. I slept through the day. I kept going all night.

ROBBIE: She was incredible.

LOELIA: If I saw anything in jeans, I fucked it.

ROBBIE: Yeah, well . . .

(*He loses his thread.* LOELIA *realizes, and tries to backtrack. Quietly:*)

LOELIA: No, sorry, you say.

(ROBBIE *smiles sheepishly.*)

ROBBIE: Well, I met her because my father got a lot of letters. About this and that. So I was intrigued by the coincidence that I was doing my postgraduate degree at the same college. She was a sophomore. I went and watched her in the canteen.

LOELIA: I never noticed.

ROBBIE: No, well you were always in shades. This was lunchtime. And one day I finally plucked up courage, took over my chipped steak. I toyed with it. She said, 'I'd like to go out with you.' 'With me? With *me*? You're crazy.' Hoping, of course. I said, 'I've seen the people you go out with.' She said, 'I've had enough of them. I don't want any more cowboy boots.' (*He smiles.*) My heart was beating, I was red, I felt my face was red, I could feel my heart pounding. I said, 'How do you know? How do you know

73

I'm not a cowboy boot?' She said, 'You're not.' I said,
'What am I?' She said, 'You're what I need. You're a
brown shoe.'

(*There is an appreciative silence.*)

LOELIA: That's right.

GRACE: Huh.

LOELIA: I'd forgotten that.

ROBBIE: About the *shoe*?

LOELIA: No, about the chipped steak.

ROBBIE: You had yoghurt.

LOELIA: Healthy, you see. Drugged out, but healthy. Never
took drugs again. (*She nods.*) You see, it's interesting. This
man changed me. Bang, just like that. It happens. (*She
shakes her head.*) I thought I knew who I was.

ROBBIE: And I reaped the benefit. You see I didn't . . . let's be
frank . . . the kind of person you were is not the kind I'm
normally attracted to. But I made an exception. And it
worked out real well.

GRACE: What about your father?

ROBBIE: Mmm?

GRACE: You mentioned, it was started by this letter she wrote.
Did he ever answer it?

(ROBBIE *is suddenly absent.*)

ROBBIE: I have no idea.

(GRACE *looks at him a moment.*)

GRACE: I write. I've started. It's a form of obsession. I've
started writing letters. I have a false name.

ROBBIE: Oh yeah?

GRACE: Yeah.

ROBBIE: What is it?

GRACE: Amelia. Was Della Santa Cruz. But I decided that was
too ethnic.

ROBBIE: It isn't good.

GRACE: Now I'm Amelia Grant.

LOELIA: Too far the other way. It sounds too white-bread.

ROBBIE: What sort of letters? Letters to the papers?

GRACE: I mean *me*, of all people, who knows how papers work.

What they print, what they won't. What the party line is.
But when I'm Amelia, I'm free. (*She smiles.*)

ROBBIE: What sort of things? Is she political? Loelia was
political once.

GRACE: Oh sure. But she tries to be humorous–political. She
knows serious–political will never get in.

LOELIA: So she isn't quite free.

GRACE: Mezzo-mezzo. She has a point to make. She makes it in
a way which is digestible. But there's no mistaking her
passion.

ROBBIE: Is she a nutcase?

GRACE: No. She's just angry.

ROBBIE: Why?

GRACE: Why would you be angry?
(*She looks at him, but he simply looks lost.*)
Because there are no movies. Because the blacks can't get
jobs . . .

ROBBIE: Oh, I know this woman.

GRACE: No, you don't. You don't know this woman. You think
you do. But she's smarter than you are.

ROBBIE: Does she write about bussing?

GRACE: Her big thing is fantasy. Yeah. She attacks it. The idea
that everyone can have what they want. She says they can't.
She's always writing about exercise class. She says fat
people are fat. They'll never look like movie stars. It's cruel
to pretend to them they can. And of course it's the movie
stars themselves who make the money by encouraging that
delusion. By selling their fantasy videos. The women
should live with their fatness. Just try to come to terms
with it.

ROBBIE: She sounds a pain in the ass. (*He grins, then backs off.*)
No, really. I think she's wrong.

GRACE: That's your right. Write a letter.

ROBBIE: There's no point.

GRACE: Well, of course I feel that. You feel that. *People* feel
that. But Amelia doesn't. About so many things. That's
why I like her.

LOELIA: She cares.

(ROBBIE *looks rather indignant.*)

ROBBIE: Cares about *what*? I don't get it. She doesn't care. She disagrees. She dissents. That's her privilege. It's also our privilege to ignore her. And get on with our lives.

LOELIA: Is that right?

ROBBIE: Yes, it is. (*He shakes his head.*) Fuck Amelia. Frankly. I like Grace. (*He smiles at her.*) Why do you need the pseudonym? Are you ashamed?

GRACE: No. I feel helpless. Don't you ever feel helpless? Like, at the moment my life is in real estate. I'm working for a developer. He's one of the most powerful men in New York. Tiny office, dark suits, forty. His wife, his oldest son, and his secretary. That's his whole staff. And from his two-room office, he's trying to tear down twelve blocks on the West Side of New York. (*She sweeps with her arm.*) Docks are going to go. And houses. There's a park. There are shops. There are old apartment buildings. What we call *life*, in fact, that's what he's planning to remove. And in its place . . . you can imagine . . . you've seen it before he's even built it, it's dark, it's brutal, it's brown. It's eighty storeys of air-conditioned nothing. Great subdivided sections of air full of profit. For no conceivable human purpose at all.

(ROBBIE *is about to interrupt, but* GRACE *anticipates.*)

All right, that's it, that's OK, let's say it's not even to be argued with. It's progress. He comes to *me*. He says, of course I hate personal publicity. I say, who doesn't? It's a given. It's why film stars ride in thirty-foot black limos – to be inconspicuous. It's why they have loud voices in restaurants, and employ people like me. Because they hate publicity so much. 'What do you want,' I said, 'a new image? People to like you? A positive slant on all this?' 'Oh no,' he said 'I just need a black fireball of controversy. That way things will just burn themselves out.' (*She leans forward.*) And he's *clever*, you see. He's not frightened. He understands the process. We go for the cover of a New

76

York magazine. 'The loathsome face of a property developer!' And inside it says 'But he gives money to charity.' So he's what magazines call 'complex'. He's got two sides to him. Well! He attends his children's school play. And people eat this crap, they love it, it's called personality. He's an asshole, *but*. What is he like? What is he like? is the only question. The question is never 'Is this right or wrong?' (*She shakes her head, suddenly vehement.*) It's not 'Shall we do this?' 'Should this be done?' No, it's 'Do we like the guy who's doing this? Is he a nice guy?' Not even nice, is he good copy? Then, hell, let him do what he wants. He wants a concentration camp for millionaires on the West Side? Let him have it. He's an interesting person. Forget the people who live on those blocks right now. They have no personality. They'll never make the cover. So they must be moved out of the way.

(*There is a pause.*)

ROBBIE: (*Thoughtful*) I can see what you're saying. I think it's kind of pointless.

LOELIA: She feels it, Robbie.

ROBBIE: So?

LOELIA: Respect that.

ROBBIE: I do respect it. However, I also happen to think that she's wrong.

(GRACE *smiles, unfazed.*)

GRACE: In what way?

ROBBIE: There's nothing you can do. That's how people see things.

GRACE: Not people. Americans.

ROBBIE: Well, Americans are people, for Christ's sake. They're people.

(*He awaits a response.*)

GRACE: Of course.

ROBBIE: We're people. We are people. Like any other people.

GRACE: Not quite like.

ROBBIE: (*Frowns*) Anyway, in this case I sort of think people are right.

LOELIA: What do you mean?

ROBBIE: 'What's he like?' *is* the most important question. Like, say, when you fall in love, it's not because of what the other person *does*. Or else, you know, Mother Teresa would be the most propositioned woman on the planet. Because what she *does* is unbeatable. But that's got nothing to do with what draws people to people.

GRACE: Well, yeah, but that's different. That's in your private life.

ROBBIE: I don't think so. No, it's in everything. Nobody's interested in what people do. I'm a lawyer, for instance, I watch juries. You think they're judging the case? No, of course not. They're deciding if they like and therefore trust the defendant. They're judging the person.

GRACE: Well . . .

ROBBIE: Aren't they?

GRACE: In part. (*She begins to get flustered.*) I mean, yes. Of course. Don't tell me. I understand your argument. (*She smiles.*) I'm dating the son. I was. The man I just got pregnant by, he's the son of this property developer.

ROBBIE: I see.

(*There is a pause.*)

Oh, I see.

GRACE: Well, exactly. He does half the deals. I'm not altogether clear on this either. (*She smiles across at* LOELIA.)

ROBBIE: Well, I mean, you're not giving him up because of his business ethics . . .

GRACE: No.

ROBBIE: It's not a gesture of disgust. Because his father is destroying Manhattan.

GRACE: No, I'm 'giving him up', as you say, because he gets angry. And I get resentful and hopeless and dishonest. I know. I admit that. Let's face it. That's fine. But apart from all that, I also feel there has to be a line.

ROBBIE: A line?

GRACE: Yes. There has to be something . . . I don't know . . . some *standard*. Which unfortunately it is usually my professional duty to disguise.

ROBBIE: Come on, that's ridiculous.

GRACE: If there isn't what are we? I mean, is there nothing? Is everything allowed?

(*There is a pause.*)

Well, is it?

ROBBIE: You mean, like, would I go out with a murderess?

GRACE: Yes. If you like.

(*There is a pause.*)

LOELIA: Would you?

ROBBIE: I don't know. Maybe. (*He attempts a self-conscious joke.*) If I thought we'd have a good time.

(*At once* LOELIA *begins to get angry with him.*)

LOELIA: I don't know how you say that. You simply can't say that. And be serious.

ROBBIE: Well, I only want to go out with you. In fact. If we're talking *serious* . . .

LOELIA: Now, Robbie . . .

ROBBIE: *That's* the dishonesty. I don't know why you're so desperate to split.

(LOELIA *gets up at once to head towards the hall.* ROBBIE *has already got up from the sofa in sudden indignation.*)

LOELIA: I have to get out of this, I'm sorry . . .

GRACE: Loelia, please don't go.

LOELIA: Robbie, you made me a promise.

ROBBIE: I know. (*A pause. Then quietly:*) I just broke it.

LOELIA: We agreed. No mention of that subject. That was the deal. That's the only reason I stayed on for this – what's your name for it?

GRACE: He said 'rite of passage'.

LOELIA: That's it.

(ROBBIE *has turned calmly to* GRACE.)

ROBBIE: You see, it's at Loelia's wish we're parting.

LOELIA: Robbie, please.

ROBBIE: Well, it is.

(LOELIA *glowers at him.*)

I can say that. Please. I would imagine Grace has already spotted that. I thought we wanted our feelings out in the open.

LOELIA: No. You wanted that. Because you have nothing to
lose.
(*There is a silence.* GRACE *is embarrassed by the sudden
intensity of feeling. Neither of them now seems inclined to
speak.*)

GRACE: Mmm, yes, well . . .

ROBBIE: Huh.
(GRACE *speaks suddenly, after a pause.*)

GRACE: And Coca-Cola.

ROBBIE: What?

GRACE: No, earlier we were saying, it just occurred to me, we
were talking about contraception, that's all . . .

ROBBIE: Oh yes.

GRACE: Did you know that in Third World countries people use
Coke as a douche?

ROBBIE: I hadn't heard that.

LOELIA: (*Sour*) It's true.

GRACE: Yeah. They ran tests at Harvard Medical School. To
choose between all the different brands.

ROBBIE: Oh really?

GRACE: Yeah. Classic Coke. New Coke. Caffeine-free. Diet.
They finally proved Diet Coke is the best.

ROBBIE: I like it best.

GRACE: Yeah. I mean sure, yeah. I *like* it. But it's also the most
effective spermicide.

ROBBIE: I see.

GRACE: It's a fact. They're dead in an hour.

ROBBIE: (*Grins*) I'll remember that.

GRACE: Yeah.
(LOELIA *is now sitting at the back of the room by herself.*
ROBBIE *throws a nervous look at her, but she does not
respond.*)
Scientists say they can't even get a Journal of Negative
Results. This thing about success, it's even in science. You
follow a line of research. Well, if the conclusions are
negative, scientists are saying they can't even get the results
published. You *didn't* come up with a cure for cancer? Oh

well, fuck off, we don't want to know. (*She shakes her head.*) I mean this is science we're talking about. Which is meant to proceed by trial and error. Only now no one's interested in error. It's bad ju-ju. That's what I mean about the worship of success.

ROBBIE: Oh I see. Yeah. (*He frowns.*) No, that's right. But I mean surely . . .

GRACE: It's like we're all set on the elimination of pain. We're all meant to pretend it just doesn't happen. Well, it does. Life isn't a Woody Allen movie. Things don't come out right. Finally all stories end badly.

ROBBIE: What? (*He looks at her, puzzled.*) What d'you mean?

GRACE: Well . . . (*She looks to* LOELIA *now, embarrassed at having to explain.*) I mean, I don't mean to be over-obvious . . . (*She pauses.*)

ROBBIE: I still don't get it.

LOELIA: She means all stories end when we die.

(LOELIA'*s voice from the back is clear, almost like a nurse.* ROBBIE *frowns.*)

ROBBIE: Well, I mean, sure. Hey, that's a hard one. Whoo. You threw me for a loop there.

GRACE: I'm sorry. No, I . . .

ROBBIE: Hey, that's pretty heavy. That's a pretty heavy thought. I'm not sure I know what to do with that one.

GRACE: No. (*She smiles.*) Well, most people don't.

ROBBIE: Let's be clear: you can't think about that every day. Else you'd go crazy. It's very negative. That's what I don't like about death. This idea that everything's negative.

(*He sits, thoughtful, pained, then without a word he suddenly gets up and goes out of the front door. There is a pause.* LOELIA *is at the table,* GRACE *still in her chair.*)

LOELIA: I think he's gone for a swim.

(*Neither of them move.*)

Would you like one?

GRACE: No. Did I offend him?

LOELIA: What? Oh no.

GRACE: He went very quiet.

81

LOELIA: No. It wasn't that. It was because of your pseudonym. You hit on something. Accidentally. (*Something catches her eye out of the window. She frowns, annoyed.*)

He's got no clothes on.

GRACE: Where?

LOELIA: In the pool.

GRACE: Oh, really?

LOELIA: Fuck him. *He* wears no clothes, that's what's unfair. He gets so angry with me. I hate wearing clothes. He says I have to. People expect it.

GRACE: Sure. Tennis lessons.

(*She smiles, but* LOELIA *is lost in thought as if looking at* ROBBIE *for the first time.*)

LOELIA: You should come and look.

GRACE: No, I couldn't.

LOELIA: He looks so . . . childlike. He never gets that. That that's what I love in him.

GRACE: Then why are you leaving?

(LOELIA *pauses a moment.*)

LOELIA: Years ago he changed his name.

GRACE: Ah.

(LOELIA *looks down.*)

Oh, I see. Why?

LOELIA: Why did he change it?

GRACE: Yes.

LOELIA: Because it was Dvořák.

GRACE: Dvořák?

LOELIA: Yes.

(*There is a pause.*)

Like I said.

GRACE: You mean like the composer?

LOELIA: No. Not the composer. Dvořák. More like the spy.

(*There is an oblivious cry of excitement from the pool. And the sound of a splash.*)

ROBBIE: (*Off*) Come on in everybody.

LOELIA: He's not Robbie Baker. He's the son of Bill Dvořák. Remember? There are so many ironies. Like Robbie's

82

profession. You would think with his father in the law court for so long the last thing he'd want is to be a lawyer. He's a prosecutor. (*She shrugs.*) I shouldn't tell you. I never know who he tells, like his chiropractor knows. God knows why.

GRACE: Do his partners in the firm?

LOELIA: (*Shakes her head*) He says his chiropractor knows everything about him. He has a very bad back.

GRACE: (*Thoughtful*) Bill Dvořák.

LOELIA: Yeah, exactly. (*There is a long silence.*) Now you begin to see who he is.

(*At once* ROBBIE *returns. He is in a big white towelling robe and is very invigorated.*)

ROBBIE: That was great. Hey. Come on. Who's going to join me?

GRACE: No thanks.

ROBBIE: I built the pool myself from a kit. Now when I swim, I think 'Hey, I earned this, I put in the work.'

LOELIA: I have to cook. (*She turns to go out to the kitchen.*)

ROBBIE: Have you been talking about me?

GRACE: No. She was admiring your body.

LOELIA: Please Grace, keep confidence. (*She's gone.*)

GRACE: It's all right. Don't worry. I didn't look.

(ROBBIE *smiles as he rubs his head with a towel to dry his hair.* GRACE *gets up, frowning.*)

ROBBIE: No, I don't mind. I think there's too much prudishness. We're all the same. Don't you think?

GRACE: No. (*She has crossed the room and bent down under a chair to pick up a large plastic dinosaur.*)

ROBBIE: You seem very certain.

GRACE: What's this?

ROBBIE: Oh, it's Danny's. I'll clear it out the way.

(*At once he puts it in a trunk at the side of the room. The only untidy object has gone. He throws a cloth on to the table and begins to lay places.*)

GRACE: I did a nude beach. I mean, I did the publicity. It was on Long Island. It was called Bare Glare. It was naturist chic. I had to sit and do business with the guy who ran it.

In his office. He was Latvian. Around sixty. He was into
high-tech. Bare floors. Glass tables. He sat behind his desk
in a Corbusier chair. With a great stainless steel lamp, like a
hairdryer on the end of a fishing rod, shining down on him.
And I sit there thinking, where do I look?

(ROBBIE *smiles and goes out.* GRACE *gets up to speak loud
enough to be heard in the kitchen.*)

Through the glass top . . . I'm sitting opposite . . . I can
see his whole . . . thing. It's sort of lolling there, while he
talks budgets and ad-rates, and can we re-route the Jitney?
I mean, then he's up and he's standing at the filing cabinet.
All I'm getting is this little scraggy ass, and he's pulling out
statistics, and I think, what the fuck's going on? (*She stands
in the middle of the room, genuinely bewildered.*) Is it just me?
Am I the only one who sees this? Am I the only one who
thinks, hold on a moment, is this normal? Does anyone else
see this? Or am I alone?

ROBBIE: (*Kitchen*) Sure.

GRACE: Everyone behaves as if everything's normal. And yet to
me, everything's strange. (*She looks round the room as if it
were further evidence of what she's saying.*) I feel that. I feel it
in the butcher's. Little heaps of money changing hands
behind your back. You think, what is this? I go in the other
day for veal chops. In comes this very short guy. Says,
here's the money for you, Frank. Oh thank you, the
money. Hands him what looks like *two thousand dollars*.
You think, what money, Frank? What for? Am I missing
out on something here? Is the short guy eating whole herds
of cows? Shit, I don't know. I get scared. Frank winks at
me, as if this were a joke. As if I understood. And I *don't*.
(ROBBIE *returns with a board full of cheeses, as well as platters
of seafood.*)

ROBBIE: Oh yeah, I get that. Sure. I think a lot of the time
people are surprised. They just don't like to say so. Because
it's uncool. Like we have a really bad actor for President.
(*He stops a moment.*) I mean, wait a minute. He was really
bad. What's he doing as President?

84

GRACE: That's right.

ROBBIE: No. I know. I get that feeling as well. (*He gestures to the spread.*) Clams on the half-shell. Welfleet Oysters.

GRACE: Oh, thank you.

ROBBIE: Roquefort. Brie. Dolcelatte. There's a dip.

GRACE: Wonderful.

(ROBBIE *stands a moment.*)

ROBBIE: Oh, this is going to be great. It's been great already. I'm glad it's just us. No, I . . . I said I wanted lots of people but really it was just . . . you know, I thought if there's lots of people, I won't fall apart.

GRACE: Well, there's just me. So go easy.

ROBBIE: Oh. Sure. No. Don't worry. I've had my breakdown about this. I'm going to a really smart shrink. He said, it's never a breakdown, it's always a breakthrough.

GRACE: Huh.

(*He stands, thinking.* GRACE *is tentative; after a pause:*) And what . . . I mean . . . would you say that was true?

ROBBIE: True? (*He looks startled. Then quietly:*) Yeah, well, it's helpful. It's a good way to look at things.

GRACE: But is it true?

(*She waits, then seeing the look in his eye, she retreats.*) I'm sorry. It's none of my business.

(*He's staring at her.*)

ROBBIE: Did she talk to you? Loelia?

GRACE: Well . . .

ROBBIE: Goddammit, I know she did. I can tell she did.

(*There is a pause.*)

GRACE: Yes.

ROBBIE: You know who I was.

(*He looks at her. Then in the silence, he moves across and sits down at the half-laid table.*)

GRACE: Yes, look, please. It doesn't matter. I'll pretend it was never said. Honestly.

ROBBIE: No.

(*She waits a moment, but he says no more.*)

GRACE: I remember the trial.

(ROBBIE *just looks at her.*)

I liked your dad. He seemed principled.

ROBBIE: Really?

GRACE: He did what he did because he believed the two sides should be equal. That they should know the same things.

(ROBBIE *doesn't answer.*)

No, well, probably you get sick of discussing it.

ROBBIE: I never discuss it. It's in the past.

GRACE: It was at a very low level. That's what always struck me. When people went nuts. The things that he told – operational details of nuclear submarines – they were hardly critical.

(ROBBIE *looks across at her, level.*)

ROBBIE: You misunderstand me. I didn't like him, that's all.

(LOELIA *returns with fresh plates of food from the kitchen.*)

LOELIA: Deep sea prawns, crab sticks, this is salami from the city. (*She lays things down, then stops.*) What's wrong?

ROBBIE: No, nothing.

LOELIA: What were you talking about?

ROBBIE: My father.

LOELIA: I told her.

(*She is about to make a move of affection towards him, but he holds up a hand.*)

ROBBIE: No, it's all fine.

(LOELIA *stands behind him, quite still.*)

I disliked him as a person. That's my objection. I don't care what he *did*, as you'd say. He was a puritan. He was also a snob. He used the word 'upright'. He disapproved of how ordinary people lived. He was from Maryland, he thought himself superior. In the civil service, so he thought he knew best. How to direct peoples' lives. His contempt was astonishing. He'd walk down a street and say, these people have no culture. They watch television all day. He said, why don't people think, use their brains, read the classics? He'd analyse a problem, come to what he called a logical conclusion. He always had some expert rationale. That's why he did what he did. Because he alone understood. He

claimed to understand the need to defuse the cold war
better than anyone. And that's just about as dumb as you
can get. (*He smiles*.) That's what it taught me. Thinking
gets you nowhere. So-called thinking people do the
stupidest things. Because they live in their brains. Not in
the real world.

(*He nods.* GRACE *does not react*.)

I hated all the stupid meetings. And pamphlets. I was
paraded to idiots who thought he shouldn't go to jail. They
were so stupid they assumed I'd agree with them. That was
my childhood.

GRACE: Is he still alive?

ROBBIE: Yes. My mother died. Loelia sees him.

LOELIA: I like him. He's very sad.

ROBBIE: He's arrogant.

LOELIA: Oh sure. He still knows better all the time. Even now
he'll tell you what the government's doing wrong. But what
do you want? He should grovel? Be silent? (*She stands
behind* ROBBIE, *thoughtful, tender*.) You must allow people
some self-respect.

(ROBBIE *shows no reaction. Firm:*)

ROBBIE: My attitude is this: do something. Pay for it. Take it
like a man. Don't start squealing. If you betray your
government, fine. But be ready for the consequences. Even
if that means losing your family. The affection of your son.

GRACE: That's very bleak.

ROBBIE: I don't think about it much. (*He looks down*.) That's
why I love this country. The right to start again. The right
to acquire a new name. Cross out the past. Start over. That
seems to me a very basic thing. Well, that's what I've done.
Whatever people feel.

(*There is a pause*.)

Whatever my wife feels.

(*He stretches out a hand to* LOELIA, *which she does not take*.)

And now I think let's leave that subject alone.

LOELIA: Robbie . . .

ROBBIE: No. (*He gets up*.) I'm going to call the camp.

LOELIA: It's too early.

ROBBIE: (*Smiles at* GRACE) I miss my boy.

LOELIA: You hardly ever see him. You're always at work.

ROBBIE: That's not true.

LOELIA: Yes, it is. You tidy him away. And then go back to your work. Oh occasionally, you weep and feel lonely, and think, hey, here's the moment to talk to my boy. (*She turns to* GRACE.) Danny's just like Bill. Robbie's father.

ROBBIE: I don't see that.

LOELIA: No. (*She smiles.*) You know, I remember when I was pregnant, you had such a clear idea. 'Your son.' What your son would be. You thought it was like a restaurant. You order. You get what you want.

ROBBIE: Don't be silly.

LOELIA: No, you knew exactly.

GRACE: How old is he?

ROBBIE: Nine.

LOELIA: You could see him. You could dress him. He was going to have a baseball cap.

ROBBIE: Now you're being ridiculous.

(*He grins nervously.* LOELIA *turns and comes down near* GRACE.)

LOELIA: In fact he's quiet, he's rather academic, fair hair, reads books. Whereas Robbie loves all things American. He likes Buddy Holly. And diners. And going to the game.

ROBBIE: What's wrong with that?

LOELIA: He's the only person I know who genuinely does. Usually the people who go for that stuff are Canadian.

ROBBIE: Canadian! (*He chuckles.*) Hey, she's hitting low.

LOELIA: Well, it's true.

(*He shakes his head.*)

ROBBIE: There's no flag in you, Loelia.

LOELIA: No.

ROBBIE: (*Grins*) She's got no flag at all.

LOELIA: Robbie stands there at baseball, he's got a hot dog in one hand, he's got popcorn in the other, he's got an extra large Diet Sprite with french fries on the side, and he's shouting 'Kill the umpire'. And I think, does he mean this? This is just a charade.

ROBBIE: I like baseball. It's honest. You hit the ball. You can score. Don't hit it. You're in trouble. (*He spreads his hands, summing it all up, enjoying this with* LOELIA.) Now that's what I call a game.

LOELIA: God, I think I married a psychopath.

ROBBIE: Tennis, now tennis, is that a game? Overpaid prima donnas, saying 'Hey, I feel faint, I don't think I'll play today, I didn't get to fuck a film star last night . . .'
(*He smiles and goes towards the door.*)
I'm going to go prime the barbecue. It makes the most wonderful steaks.

LOELIA: You have to say, why are these steaks so delicious? Because Robbie put in every brick of the barbecue himself.
(ROBBIE *stands, shaking his head.*)
Will you get some crackers from the store? We're out.

ROBBIE: Can you imagine what she's like to live with?

GRACE: Yes. I can very well.
(ROBBIE *catches the sudden seriousness of her tone. He stands a moment at the door. Then goes. The two women sit a moment.*)

LOELIA: Do you want a bath?

GRACE: Oh. No, thank you.

LOELIA: There's food.
(GRACE *smiles.*)
You can have anything.

GRACE: That's very kind of you.

LOELIA: What are you thinking?

GRACE: I'm just desperate you shouldn't split up.
(*There's a pause.* LOELIA *looks at her.*)

LOELIA: That same night we met, we slept together. You won't believe this, he took me to a hotel. I said, we both have rooms on campus. He said, I want to do this properly. Proper? What's proper about a hotel? This was in South Bend, Indiana. We went to the Ramada. I remember we had the best room. A dog barked all night. We made love, over and over. The dog went on barking. And I thought, in the dark, holding him . . . this man is the son of a spy.

GRACE: Huh.

LOELIA: I liked the idea. You see, the reason spies are so cool is
because they don't depend on anyone's approval. I liked
that. Yeah. It seemed to me good. The spy doesn't ask for
help. *He* doesn't need people telling him he's a good actor.
(GRACE *smiles*.)
He does it because he believes it is right. (*She nods slightly*.)
And fuck 'em.

GRACE: That's right.

LOELIA: That's his attitude. 'I do it. Fuck you all.' (*She smiles*.)
Oh, sure I could see he was conventional, he was never
going to be hip. But I married under a misapprehension. I
had this idea. Like father, like son. (*She suddenly turns*.)
How can it be? My God, ten years ago. What was I then?
Wild. Now I look round and I think, how has this
happened? I'm trapped. With a man whose whole life is an
attempt to pretend to be someone else.

GRACE: Well . . .

LOELIA: Yes!

GRACE: Sure.

LOELIA: You can see.

GRACE: I can. It must drive you crazy.

LOELIA: America! Shit! I practically have to run the stars and
stripes up the flagpole before I'm allowed to go to the john.
(*She shakes her head*.) You know in this country there's
meant to be freedom. Freedom! Isn't that it? So why are we
now all pretending to believe the same thing? (*There's a
pause*.) Bill wasn't even a communist. He's a man who tried
to act when he saw something he considered wrong. He
thought he could *do* something. That isn't sinister, it's
completely ridiculous.

GRACE: Sure.

LOELIA: I mean, even now if you meet him, you just think this
man is absurd. He's a joke. He lives in a Baltimore suburb.
He spends hours writing to his congressman about how his
mail is steamed open. He's still so convinced of his

'personal integrity'. It's just ridiculous. As if anyone cared.

GRACE: No one cares.

LOELIA: Robbie can't be himself. At the bottom there's a hurt.
He refuses to forgive him. And I'm exhausted, that's all.
(*There's a pause.*)
Oh, of course Robbie hides it. As people grow older, their
act gets better.

GRACE: Mine gets worse.
(*They laugh at this.*)
But then I live on my own.

LOELIA: Yeah. I've got that to look forward to.

GRACE: Oh it's quite easy. I've done it for ten years. With the
odd break. You get proud. You think, oh, I do this really
well. All my friends, I go to dinner, I think, look at them,
gutless, all huddling together in bad relationships they're
frightened to leave. I think, I'm not. I'm different. I can
face solitude. I'm tougher. More honest. (*She smiles.*) It's
an illusion, of course.

LOELIA: Yeah, it's lucky I'm a Buddhist. That's going to help.

GRACE: Huh.

LOELIA: You know we've tried everything. We've been in
therapy together. We've had a marriage counsellor. We
tried living away for a while. And there's still . . .
unhappiness.

GRACE: But how? In each other?

LOELIA: Sure. We drive each other nuts.

GRACE: But . . . (*She stops.*)

LOELIA: What?

GRACE: So does everyone.

LOELIA: Like this thing about Danny. He never talks to Danny.
The whole thing's an act. Yet one day I go into his office,
they all say there was never a father who spoke more
proudly, more obsessively of his son than Robbie.
Apparently he talks about Danny all the time. But at home
it's 'Can you go into the other room, Danny? I'm working?'
(*She looks at* GRACE.) Also. He doesn't trust me. After ten
years. I have to be careful in conversation. Things I can

say, things I can't say without hurting him. God, why can't he *trust* me by now? I trust him. He can say what he likes. I trust his love. (*She is quiet, thinking hard.*)

GRACE: But last year . . .

LOELIA: Yeah . . .

GRACE: The year before, I know it was hard. But staying was worth it. Why are you saying it's not worth it now? (LOELIA *thinks.*)

LOELIA: Well, I guess. Because I'm not happy.

GRACE: Yes?

LOELIA: Shit, I was born in Milton, Nebraska. They told me I'd be happy. (*She laughs.*) I think I've got a right to do something else.

GRACE: A right?

LOELIA: Yes.

GRACE: To what?

LOELIA: I don't know. Just something. I was meant to be happy. I'm a happy sort of girl. Instead of which . . . I don't know, I'm confused, I'm angry. We have to keep moving. He has to keep working. I have to keep whacking balls round the court. When we stop, we don't know what to do. If there's a pause, if there's a silence, then we fill it. We work. We make love. (*She smiles.*) To cover the quiet bits. (*Suddenly she gets up.*) I've paced round his problems. Like a prison-yard. I've walked round for years. I know every inch of the ground. Well, can I have some new ground? Am I allowed that? Aren't I entitled? (*She stands in the middle of the room, forceful.* GRACE *smiles.*)

GRACE: Oh, yes, well sure.

LOELIA: Anyway, you know, what makes *you* – why are you so keen I should stick at it? You don't stick at it.

GRACE: No, well, I think that's why I'm so keen that you should.

LOELIA: (*Grins*) You mean do it for you? Do it for your sake?

GRACE: I like the idea of people sticking together.

LOELIA: You don't have to do it.

GRACE: That's true. (*She smiles.*) I hate this idea that we're all just sensation. In New York I get scared. 'I feel good, I don't feel good.' As if we were nothing except what we happen to be feeling at the moment.

(*The sound of a car.*)

LOELIA: Hold it, I think he's just coming back. (*She rushes to the window to look, then turns.*) What should I do?

GRACE: What d'you mean?

LOELIA: I'm supposed to leave Monday.

(GRACE *shrugs and grins.*)

GRACE: It's up to you.

LOELIA: I mean, what I don't get . . . (*She breaks off.*) Hell, he's just coming . . . I mean, what you're saying, if we are something *more*, I mean, something *more*, like what?

GRACE: Well . . .

LOELIA: No, tell me. Like *what*? Quick.

(GRACE *pauses, takes her time.*)

GRACE: I'm just saying you have certain qualities I envy. Qualities which aren't just . . . momentary.

LOELIA: Like what?

GRACE: Loyalty. Courage. Perseverance.

(*There is a pause.*)

If you don't use them, you're going to feel lousy.

(LOELIA *looks at her from across the room, moved. Then with sudden violence.*)

LOELIA: Fuck you, Grace, you've ruined my weekend.

(*At once* ROBBIE *comes through the door, oblivious, the picture of domesticity, the husband with brown bags of groceries, very cheerful.*)

ROBBIE: Hi everyone, I'm back.

LOELIA: (*Mock-girlish*) Hi, Robbie.

GRACE: Hi.

ROBBIE: You been having a good time?

GRACE: Very good.

(*He has begun to unload his brown bags.*)

ROBBIE: Crackers. And I saw these nuts. Macadamias. I hadn't seen 'em before in this jar. And I got a packet of these new eggplant-flavoured tortilla chips.

GRACE: Oh, good.

ROBBIE: I thought they might fill a gap. (*He takes bottles out.*) This is beer. They import it from China. It's the water they use makes it special. Here we are on the Eastern seaboard. And this was bottled over ten thousand miles away. I had to buy it, because the idea amused me.

LOELIA: We'll drink it amused.

ROBBIE: What? (*He stops and looks at her.*) Hello, hon, you all right?

LOELIA: Yes, I'm fine.

(*He goes on, noticing nothing.*)

ROBBIE: Look 'biscuits de Toulon'. It's just a cracker.

GRACE: (*Smiles*) I was on holiday in Greece. I went into this shop. I saw this bottle of cologne. It was actually a press agent's dream. No bullshit, no funny packaging. They sold a cologne they called *Smell*.

ROBBIE: Huh . . . we've got champagne in the refrigerator. Shall we drink that first? There are three bottles. We ought to get started.

(*He goes out, smiling at* LOELIA *as he goes. There is a long pause. The two women do not move. Then* LOELIA, *looking straight at* GRACE, *calls towards the kitchen.*)

LOELIA: Honey. I just want a word.

(*She goes out.* GRACE *stands alone. It begins to grow dark.* GRACE *turns, thoughtfully, towards us. She stands alone. Then* LOELIA *reappears at the kitchen door.*)

LOELIA: I'm staying till Tuesday.

GRACE: A.m. or p.m.?

(LOELIA *is about to answer, as the lights fade quickly. Nat King Cole repeats the final bars of 'Nature Boy' from the dark.*)